Soap's round f... cake. If it weren't... I'd think she wasn't feeling anything. I almost hate her for never taking things seriously. She seems to enjoy trouble, and it's getting to me. I can feel tears in my eyes. I don't want her to see.

The intercom buzzes on Miss Cronin's desk.

"Send them in," says Mr. Sloucher's moist voice.

Mr. Sloucher uncoils from his chair and slithers toward the window. He talks with his back to us.

"This is the last straw. I'm going to have to suspend you for two weeks, starting now!"

The bottom has just fallen out of my stomach. I wish I could just curl up some-place and disappear. Soap and her stupid ideas!

Mr. Sloucher buzzes Miss Cronin and asks her to get our parents on the phone. Poor Mom and Dad. This is going to be very tough on them. And me, too.

**Other Scholastic paperbacks
you will enjoy:**

Adorable Sunday
  Marlene Fanta Shyer

Roses
  Barbara Cohen

If This Is Love, I'll Take Spaghetti
  Ellen Conford

Hello . . . Wrong Number
  Marilyn Sachs

*How Do You Lose Those
Ninth Grade Blues?*
  Barthe DeClements

The Great Rip-Off
  Lavinia Harris

THE TROUBLE WITH SOAP

Margery Cuyler

AN
APPLE®
PAPERBACK

SCHOLASTIC INC.
New York Toronto London Auckland Sydney

ISBN 0-590-32870-0

12 11 10 9 8 7 6 5 4 3 2 1   7   5 6 7 8 9/8 0/9

Printed in the U.S.A.   06

For Maboo and "Bu,"
with love

Contents

1. Caught in the Act

"After Charlie Grimes comes out," says Soap, "the coast should be clear."

It's lunchtime, and we're standing inside the door of the empty French room, watching who's going in and out of the boys' room across the hall. Soap's clutching a box of Saran Wrap against her chest. Why did I let her talk me into this? If I get just one more detention mark, I won't make the honor roll. At Wood Valley, you get graded for behavior as well as schoolwork. They call it effort.

"Darn," says Soap. "Here comes Mr. Goldstein. He'll take forever. All he does is drink coffee."

He does take forever, or maybe it just seems that way because everything does when you're nervous. Finally he and Charlie leave, and we have our chance.

"Okay," says Soap. "Now!"

My legs wobble as I run across the hall and through the swinging door of the boys' room.

"We have to hurry," says Soap. She tears off a piece of Saran Wrap and shoves it at me. It's all stuck together. I try to smooth it out, but my fingers are trembling so much, I make it worse. Meanwhile Soap tightly covers each of the toilet bowls in the last two booths with a flat piece of Saran Wrap.

I'm beginning to shake all over, like I used to when I stole Oreos from our family cookie jar.

"Why are you taking so long, Laurie?" asks Soap. She sounds impatient. "Here, use another piece. We still have two to go."

Suddenly the lavatory door swings open. I knew this would happen. We quickly close the doors to the first two booths and sit on the toilets. My knees are quivering.

I kept telling Soap that we wouldn't be able to pull this off, but she refused to listen. As usual. At least we're wearing pants and sneakers. We could pass for boys around the ankles.

Uh-oh. I hear someone going into the last booth, then the sound of a zipper going down. *Splat.* The beautiful sound of water hitting Saran Wrap fills the room. Someone says, "Rats." Even though I'm scared,

I start giggling. I shove my head between my knees to stop it. And then I get the hiccups.

I glance quickly to my right and see water dribbling down the cuffs of some green plaid pants and a pair of loafers. Water's also on the floor. Only one person in the whole school wears green plaid pants and loafers. Mr. Donahue, our science teacher.

"Those kids . . ." he mutters. Then he bangs open the booth door and runs to the sink.

Soap bursts into giggles. I reach under the partition and grab her ankle. "Shhh," I hiss. *Hic*. Thank goodness Mr. Donahue has turned on the faucet or he'd hear us.

Someone else comes into the boys' room, and Mr. Donahue dashes back into the booth and closes the door. He must look a mess if he doesn't want anyone to see him.

Whoever has come in walks over to my booth and jiggles the door. I hold my breath.

"Oh, sorry." It's a man's voice. Our second victim *would* have to be a teacher! He goes into the booth next to Mr. Donahue's.

I want to run, but I'm too scared.

"Of all the. . . ." Oh, no, it's the voice of Mr. Krimsky, our math teacher. He's probably the strictest teacher in the whole school.

"The same thing happened to me, George," calls Mr. Donahue weakly over the partition.

"Is that you, Mike?" asks Mr. Krimsky.

"Uh-huh," says Mr. Donahue in a small voice.

"This is really something. Even my kids wouldn't pull a stunt like this. Brad Bell's out sick today, so it couldn't be one of his wild antics. Lucinda Sokoloff and Laurie Endersby couldn't have gotten in here."

Lucinda is Soap's real name. She's called Soap because she used to watch a lot of soap operas on TV. She's always been the dramatic type.

"Mmmm. I'm not so sure."

I hear this thoughtful silence.

Soap's sweaty hand reaches under the partition. I grab it and hold on to it for dear life. It's shaking. Soap explodes into giggles. I know she can't help it, but I gesture wildly at her under the partition. She snorts as she tries to control herself. I begin to shake again, since now I *know* we're in big trouble.

Eyes bore into the top of my head. I look up and see two red faces staring down at me. Mr. Donahue and Mr. Krimsky must be standing on the toilet seats!

"Just as I thought," says Mr. Krimsky. "Come on, the four of us are going to Mr. Sloucher's office. But first I want to put a warning sign on these two booths."

"It was an accident," says Soap. "We didn't do it. I can explain everything."

How can Soap be calm at a moment like this?

"I can't *wait* to hear about it," says Mr. Krimsky, as he grabs her shoulder and shoves her toward the door.

As we walk out of the boys' room, Art Buckland walks in. I could die. He is the most popular boy in the eighth grade.

2. Mr. Sloucher's Punishment

Soap and I are marched down the corridor to the principal's office. Everyone looks at us and snickers. Mike Fragola whispers to Robin Glasser; then they both giggle. Mrs. Bushby, the gym teacher, shakes her head as she trots by in her running shoes. I wish I were invisible. I turn my head to the wall so I don't have to see them. I could kill Soap.

Mr. Sloucher's secretary, Miss Cronin, rolls her eyes to the ceiling when she sees us walk in. I feel about two inches tall. This isn't the first time we've been hauled in to confess some horrible crime.

"We'd like to talk to Hank," says Mr. Krimsky.

"Is he here?" asks Mr. Donahue.

"Just a second," says Miss Cronin.

Her stockings make a *swish-swish* sound as she waddles to the door of Mr. Sloucher's office.

She chugs back and says, "Mr. Sloucher would like to see you and Mike alone first."

So, while they're in with Mr. Sloucher, telling him the awful truth, Soap and I sit in Miss Cronin's office.

Soap's round face is as flat as a pancake. If it weren't for the glint in her eyes, I'd think she wasn't feeling anything. I almost hate her for never taking things seriously. She seems to enjoy trouble, and it's getting to me. I can feel tears in my eyes. I don't want her to see.

The intercom buzzes on Miss Cronin's desk.

"Send them in," says Mr. Sloucher's moist voice.

Mr. Sloucher's office is dingy. The furniture's old and the fluorescent lights on the ceiling give everything a sickish hue. Including Mr. Sloucher. He has this repulsive way of parting his hair. He starts the part by his ear, then plasters his few wisps of oily hair across the bald spot on top of his scalp.

"I understand you girls placed Saran Wrap over the toilet bowls in the boys' room. Now, what possessed you to do such a disgusting and destructive thing?"

Soap clears her throat. Then she says, "We've heard a lot of complaints lately about the unsanitary conditions in the boys' bathroom. So we thought that during lunch today, we'd clean it up. We put Saran Wrap over the toilet bowls to keep them from getting dirty when we stood on them to wash the ceiling."

A likely story! Sometimes Soap's last-minute explanations work, but this one is off the wall.

Mr. Sloucher uncoils from his chair and slithers toward the window. He talks with his back to us.

"I don't believe you. It's a well-known April Fools' trick to cover toilet bowls with Saran Wrap. This 'good deed' of yours is the last straw. I'm going to have to suspend you for two weeks, starting now!"

The bottom has just fallen out of my stomach. What will my parents say? They've had conferences with my teachers before about my behavior, but things have never been this bad. I've never been suspended. I wish I could just curl up someplace and disappear. Soap and her stupid ideas! I look over at her. She's looking at Mr. Sloucher. Her eyes are snapping with anger.

"I think you're being unfair," she says hotly. "We didn't do anything that bad."

"That's enough, young lady. Maybe this will knock some sense into you."

I wish it would! That would solve my problems.

Mr. Sloucher buzzes Miss Cronin and asks her to get our parents on the phone. Poor Mom and Dad. This is going to be very tough on them. And me, too.

3. Mom and Dad

"Oh, Pumpkin, why did you do it?" asks Mom as she drives me home. Napoleon, our Newfoundland dog, fills up the backseat of our yellow Volvo.

I'd like to tell Mom about Soap. About how she has this way of making me do things. But Mom wouldn't understand. She has the same problem with Dad. She does everything he wants.

Napoleon is breathing down my neck. His saliva is blowing everywhere. Mom likes all the windows open when she drives. All that fresh air.

"It was just a joke," I say. "We didn't think Mr. Sloucher would suspend us, for goodness' sake. I wish Dad didn't have to find out."

Napoleon leans forward with a goofy dog smile on his face and sticks his head out the window.

"What are you so happy about?" I ask him grumpily.

"What?" asks Mom.

"Oh, nothing. I was talking to Napoleon."

Mom steps on the brakes just in time to miss a mail truck. She's always been a terrible driver. She doesn't keep her mind on it. I look over at her. Her glasses, which have been held together by a safety pin for more than a month now, are perched on the bridge of her delicate nose. Her thick blonde hair is falling out of the clip at the back of her head. People say we look alike. Except I don't wear glasses.

"I've never understood how your father and I could produce two such different children."

Typical. Always comparing me to my brother Jonah. I thought she and Dad would stop doing that after Jonah left for college. But no way.

"He's always had lots of friends. But you just have Soap. It's not healthy, Laurie. Why don't you make some new friends?"

If Mom only knew how much I'd like to. But no one wants me. Everyone's sick of Soap and me and our dumb pranks.

"It's not as easy as you think," I say.

Mom sighs as she turns sharply into our

driveway. She comes to a gravelly halt by the kitchen door. I can tell by the way she slams the car door that she's angrier than she's letting on. I follow her up the steps and into the kitchen. She puts the kettle on for coffee.

"When are you going to tell Dad?" I ask.

"As soon as he gets home," says Mom. "I don't want to bother him at the office."

"I'm going up to my room."

"Wait," says Mom. "Don't you have a piano lesson today?"

"Do I have to go?" Even though I've practiced, I don't see how I can concentrate on a lesson.

"Mmmmm," says Mom as she reaches for some crackers on the top grocery shelf.

"Can't you call Mrs. Raymond and tell her I'm sick?"

Mom looks at me sideways and chews on her index finger. She always does this when she can't make up her mind.

"Well . . . maybe you shouldn't have to go after all."

"Will you call her?"

Mom sighs. "Oh, all right. I guess it won't hurt to miss your lesson just this once."

"Thanks." I rush over to give her a hug, but she pulls away.

"Go along now. I have a lot to do this afternoon."

She's still upset or else she'd hug me.

I drag myself up the stairs to my room and collapse on the bed. I feel totally alone. It's going to be a long afternoon waiting for Dad to come home.

"Laurie!" Dad's voice pounds into my head.

I wake up with a jolt, then remember why this sense of dread is hanging over me. Dad hates it when I burst his image of how an ideal daughter's supposed to act.

Maybe if I change into the kilt he gave me last Christmas, he won't be so mad. He says it shows off my long legs, which, personally, I think look like a flamingo's. Anyway, I put it on and rush into the bathroom to brush my teeth. I put baby powder on the hair near my scalp so it won't look quite so dirty. I also have two pimples on my chin, which I cover with some of my mother's powder. I put one last dab of powder on my biggest pimple and go downstairs.

I feel Dad's anger the minute I walk into the living room. He's sitting on the couch, straightening up the magazines on the coffee table in front of him. His normally neat hair is tousled — probably because Mom drove him home from the train station. He doesn't look at me. Mom's sitting next to him in her crazy pink sweater — the one that makes her look like some college kid. Her gray eyes worriedly travel between Dad and me.

I want to cry, but I blink my eyes to hold back the tears. The best way to deal with Dad is to keep a cool head. Maybe because he's a lawyer.

Finally Dad says, "Your mother told me about your latest trick. I don't see how you could be stupid enough to think you could get away with such a thing. Why did you do it?"

My lips are trembling so much it's hard to answer.

"I don't know," I say weakly. Dad's only interested in my doing well, not in *why* I sometimes don't.

"You don't know?" Dad gets up and starts walking back and forth like some caged lion. "Well, you'd better figure it out, because I won't put up with any more of this. I've reached the end of my rope."

I look down at my feet.

Dad's quiet for a while. Then he purses his lips and says, "And another thing. Why did Mr. Sloucher suspend you for *two* whole weeks? That seems awfully severe."

Phew. At least he's not 100 percent on Mr. Sloucher's side.

"I don't know," I say again.

"Is that all you can say? 'I don't know'? You've certainly acquired an extensive vocabulary at that school."

Now I really feel like crying. I hate it when Dad gets sarcastic.

He takes out his handkerchief and blows his nose. It seems to calm him down. Then he says, "I need to talk to your mother alone. Would you go out to the kitchen for a minute?"

I try to hear what they're saying by putting my ear against the kitchen door, but they're talking in blurry whispers. Naturally, Mom's going to agree with whatever Dad suggests.

After five awful minutes, Dad tells me to come back into the living room.

I stand in front of Mom and Dad, expecting the worst.

Dad clears his throat. "We've decided," he says, "to ground you for the two weeks you're suspended. We hope that next time you'll think twice before agreeing to do something you'll regret later on. For the next two weeks, you're not allowed to make or receive phone calls, play with friends, or watch television!"

I glare at Mom. She looks at me helplessly, as if she wishes she were out in her garden instead of in the living room having to deal with me. I go to where she's sitting and put my arms around her shoulders.

"I really am sorry," I say.

"I know, Pumpkin."

She stands up and hugs me. She's forgiven me, thank goodness. She feels like a great big hot-water bottle. I put my head on her shoulder and begin to cry. It all comes out, finally. The tears feel good, rolling down my cheeks. I think about Soap and wonder if she has ever cried on her mother's shoulder.

4. Midnight Meeting

"Pssst, Laurie."

I can't believe it. It's almost midnight. Soap's round face is staring in the window at me. Napoleon leaps off the bed and dashes toward her. His hackles rise, and he growls. Good grief, all I need is for Mom and Dad to wake up. How can Soap do this to me? Especially after today. Doesn't she understand anything?

I run to the window and open it. Soap is perched on the ladder from our garage. So *that's* how she got up here.

"Go away," I hiss. "Mom and Dad are really upset. They've grounded me for two whole weeks!"

Napoleon jumps up and licks Soap's face. His tail is wagging back and forth like crazy. I grab his choke collar, and he starts to cough and wheeze.

"Calm down," I say.

"I have to talk to you," says Soap. "It's urgent. My mother is sending me to Miss Pringle's. It's the worst thing that has ever happened to me!"

I practically drop dead with shock. Nobody in her right mind would go to Miss Pringle's. It's the snobbiest school in Middletown. For a moment, I forget that I'm mad.

"She can't do that! It will ruin your life."

Napoleon finally lies down. I guess he realizes Soap's not coming in.

Soap clutches the top of the ladder dramatically and whispers, "Mr. Sloucher called Mom at work today. Naturally, she had a fit. Anything that interrupts her work makes her angry. I had to take a taxi home. Then, between meetings, Mom called me and told me that my getting suspended confirmed her feeling that Wood Valley is an awful school. She's making me take the entrance exams for Miss Pringle's on Friday. That's the day after *tomorrow*! We've got to do something. I'd *hate* Miss Pringle's."

Soap's voice rises as she finishes telling me this awful piece of news.

"Shhhh. Keep your voice down." I want to strangle her. I'm terrified my parents might wake up and hear us. They would probably disown me. I have to get rid of her. Except that I want to hear more. Why does Soap always make me feel as though I'm being pulled two ways at once?

"What does your father think?" I whisper.

"I don't know. Mom couldn't reach him. He's in Boston, working on another bug — termites. But he's coming home tomorrow."

Mr. Sokoloff is a science writer who goes through phases. Last year, it was fleas. This year, it's termites. He's the distracted type. Vague, as Soap puts it.

"You've got to talk to him and make him understand that you don't want to go. Maybe he can change your mother's mind."

"No way. You know my mother. Once she decides something, there's nothing you can do."

Soap's mother is weird. She never pays attention to Soap unless there's some catastrophe. And then, instead of punishing her, she comes up with some wacky idea. Like sending her to Miss Pringle's. Sometimes I wish she *would* punish Soap.

Suddenly I hear a door open down the hall.

Napoleon thumps his tail against the floor.

"Napoleon, cool it!"

I frantically grab him and pull him toward the bed.

"Someone's coming," I hiss at Soap. She ducks and I jump into bed. Phew. Just in time. Dad pokes his head into the room. He comes over and kisses me on the forehead. I guess he's forgiven me, too. If Soap wasn't here, I'd "wake up" and talk to him. But I can't. I want to scream. I'm scared he'll see the ladder. Luckily, he stays only for a few seconds. Then he goes into the bathroom before shuffling back to his and Mom's room.

When the coast is clear, I tiptoe quickly to the window.

"You've got to get out of here. Right now!" I practically push Soap down the ladder.

"Okay. Okay, I'm leaving. But I want you to promise me something."

I'd promise anything just to make her leave.

"What?"

"I want you to promise me you'll apply to Miss Pringle's, too."

"Are you out of your mind?"

"You *have* to. It's the *only* way I'll survive!"

"I can't do that!"

"Will you at least think about it? *Please?*"

"Okay. Okay, but hurry up."

I breathe a sigh of relief as Soap gets the ladder back in the garage. Then she turns and waves before disappearing into the bushes of Mr. Thompson's house next door.

Napoleon comes over and takes my hand in his mouth. He wants me to get back in bed so he can get some sleep. Sometimes I think he's part human.

I can't sleep. All I can think about is Miss Pringle's. It might be good for Soap and me to spend some time apart. So, how come I don't feel happy she's applying? It makes me feel I have a hole inside. Maybe I'd miss her and her crazy ideas. Maybe I'd like Miss Pringle's more than I think. It's supposed to have good teachers. And none of the kids would know about my terrible past. I might even make some new friends. Except that the Miss Pringle's girls I met playing field hockey were terrible. They acted like they were in the Olympics or something. All concentration and no fun. But Jonah says you have to try new things; otherwise life is boring. I wish I knew what to do. I know one thing. Soap's counting on me. She'll kill me if I don't apply.

I decide to talk to Mom and Dad about it at breakfast. See what they think.

I curl up next to Napoleon's warm body and finally get to sleep.

5. Miss Pringle

The next morning, Mom swings through the kitchen door with a pot of oatmeal in her hands, some napkins tucked under her chin, and a large wooden spoon in her mouth.

"Wohl woo unsquabble deez tings?" she asks.

"What?" says Dad.

Mom plunks everything down on the table.

"Will you unscramble these things," she asks, "while I get the orange juice?"

"I'll do it," I say. "But why do we have to have oatmeal *again*? This is the fifth day in a row."

"There was a special on it at the A&P. Make yourself some toast if you don't want to eat it. This afternoon I'll make the rest into oatmeal cookies."

"Yum," says Dad. Then he smacks his

lips like some kid in a cereal commercial. Honestly. Dad acts so goofy sometimes.

After we sit down, I say, "I've been thinking about something."

"Oh?" Mom looks a little worried.

I push the oatmeal around in my bowl. "I've been thinking . . . maybe I'd be happier if I changed schools."

There's this big silence. Dad and Mom exchange looks. Finally, Dad says, "Go on."

"I'm . . . getting tired of Wood Valley School. What Mom says is true. Soap is my only friend there. And I've heard the teachers are better at Miss Pringle's."

Dad lays down his spoon and carefully wipes his mouth with his napkin. "We thought about sending you kids to private school a long time ago. But then we decided it would be a good experience for you to go to public school. We thought you'd meet a greater cross section of people. And certainly public school didn't hurt Jonah. He got into Dartmouth."

Why'd he have to mention Jonah? Can't we have one discussion without Jonah coming into it? I love him and everything, but it's hard to follow in the footsteps of an older brother who's brilliant.

"I'm not sure an all-girls school is such a great idea," adds Mom. "I went to one for seventeen years, and that's why it's taken me so long to feel natural in mixed company." Mom looks at Dad and laughs. "Your father was different. I always felt wonderful around him."

Sometimes I wish Mom wasn't so in love with Dad. Then maybe she'd pay more attention to me. I feel like Dad's first in this family, Jonah's second, and I'm third.

"I suppose we could look into Miss Pringle's again," says Dad. "Only we haven't budgeted any money for it."

Phew. Maybe I won't have to go after all. It's weird. Part of me wants to go and part of me doesn't.

I go over what Mom and Dad have just said. Then I think about Soap. I wish I knew what to do.

"Could you at least think about it?" I ask them.

"We'll talk more at dinner," says Dad. "I have to go or I'll be late." He kisses Mom's cheek and mine, and dashes out to the garage.

Mrs. Sokoloff calls Mom from work to tell her about sending Soap to Miss Pringle's.

"What a coincidence," says Mom. "Laurie was just thinking she'd like to go."

Poor Mom. If she only knew about our midnight meeting. Next I hear her asking the Sokoloffs for dinner that night to talk some more about it.

Soap's mother arrives in a black-and-blue plaid suit. Her blouse matches the blue in her suit perfectly, and her black high heels look newly polished. Naturally, not one hair is out of place. Soap's father, on the other hand, looks like a bunch of pipe cleaners knotted together. His knuckles and knees and elbows and nose are knobby, and his head looks like a marble balanced on the top of a straw.

Since I ate dinner early, I crouch on the upstairs landing, listening to them down in the dining room.

"Eighty percent of last year's graduating class was accepted by Ivy League colleges," says Mrs. Sokoloff in her rasping voice. "Miss Pringle's is clearly one of the highest ranking secondary schools in the country. And Miss Pringle is very perceptive. She thinks Soap would do well there. She says Soap needs a challenge. Of course, I've been telling Irving that for years."

Soap's father doesn't say a thing. He's probably thinking about termites. And neither of them seems to have asked Soap her opinion. But then they never do. My father doesn't say much either. It's a dull supper.

Of course, I'm dying to know what happens when Soap takes her entrance exams. Since I'm not allowed to call her, I have to wait until choir practice on Sunday morning.

Soap and I have been in the choir ever since I can remember. Singing is about the only extracurricular thing Soap likes. She is a loud soprano. I sing alto, and Mr. Whitten, our organist, says I have a great voice. At least I'm better than Jonah at something. He can't even carry a tune.

As we change into our robes, Soap says, "Miss Pringle is an old bag. She must have started that school a hundred years ago! But the exams weren't as bad as I thought. I think I did okay. I had to write about my least favorite and my favorite books on the English exam. So I picked *Harriet the Spy* as my favorite and *Cinderella* as my least favorite."

"*Cinderella*?"

"I've never liked that story. Cinderella is a wimp. If she had used her brains, she wouldn't have needed her fairy godmother."

Typical.

"What was the math like?"

"Awful. I probably failed. I hear the results on Tuesday."

"So, I guess you're going. If you pass the exams, I mean."

"Yep. You don't sound too happy about the whole thing. You *are* coming with me, aren't you?"

I bite my lower lip. "I don't know."

Soap glares at me. "What do you mean, *you don't know*?"

She buttons her robe up the wrong way, so it's crooked.

"Look, Laurie, I'm starting a week from Monday. That means your parents should talk to Miss Pringle tomorrow. You can't just sit around and expect everything to happen at the last minute." She realizes she's messed up on the buttons and practically yanks them off as she starts over.

"I don't think my father has the money," I say feebly.

"That's ridiculous. He's a lawyer, for goodness' sake. Besides, he could take out a loan, just like my parents are doing."

"But your mother works. And you don't have a brother in college."

"You're just making up excuses. If you want to go badly enough, your parents can *find* the money."

Soap's right. Anyway, it's impossible to argue with her. And the more I think about going to Miss Pringle's, the more I like the idea. Besides, I could always go back to Wood Valley if things didn't work out.

Mom and Dad aren't exactly thrilled with my decision, but they do arrange an interview for me. They can get a loan if I still want to go after seeing the school.

Mom walks with me to Miss Pringle's Tuesday morning, when I have to take the entrance exams. Instead of wearing an old pair of jeans and an enormous sweater, she's put on her best lavender suit. I'm glad she's made the effort. It would be embarrassing to be seen with her looking like some college kid.

There are girls of all ages sitting on the railing of the rambly porch that hugs the first story. They're talking in small groups as we walk by. I don't think they even notice us, but I feel conspicuous. They look like they come from one big, rich, preppy family.

Miss Pringle's office is on the second floor. It's much airier than Mr. Sloucher's, and looks out over a grove of walnut trees.

Miss Pringle greets us with a big smile. She's old, all right. But not *that* old. She looks around sixty. And has legs shaped like tree trunks.

"I'm going to take you down the hall to the library, where you can take your tests.

You'll have two hours. When you're through, I want you to come back here so that we can talk."

Mom has a strained smile on her face as she gives me a little wave.

Miss Pringle's shoes *tick-tock* on the hard wooden floors as she leads me to the library.

The English exam is a breeze, since I've already figured out my favorite and least favorite books and what I'm going to say about them. The math, history, French, and science tests are more difficult, mostly because I don't know the answers to many of the multiple-choice questions. Good grief, I bet I won't get in.

I feel sort of sick to my stomach as I walk back to Miss Pringle's office. Maybe I'm not very bright. Maybe I'm better off at Wood Valley, where everything's familiar and I know I can do well.

"I'm afraid that I didn't know the answers to a lot of the questions." I start poking at the corner of her blue carpet with my toe.

"Don't worry," says Miss Pringle. "You have a good record, and you'll catch up. What I'm more concerned about is your past behavior. Your disciplinary record from Wood Valley leaves much to be desired."

I can feel myself turning red.

"No one here will tolerate that sort of nonsense."

She smiles for just a second, and her blue eyes get lighter. "This is a very different kind of school, you know. But I think you'll like it here."

Then she asks me a few more questions about my interests, hobbies, and so on. Finally she says, "I've told your mother that she'll hear from me Thursday. You can go now."

For the next two days, I walk around with a knot in my stomach. It's awful having to wait for a decision.

But believe it or not, I get in. So does Soap. I actually got an A on the English test.

I lie awake the night before my first day, thinking about the kids I'm leaving, and the kids I'm about to meet. I hope they'll like me. This is probably the scariest thing I've done in my whole life. And all because of Soap.

6. Our First Day

On Monday morning, Mrs. Sokoloff drives Soap and me to Miss Pringle's on her way to the computer firm where she works. She picks me up a few minutes early.

"I hope you don't mind," she says. "I have a breakfast meeting this morning. It's very important." Honestly. You'd think she'd talk to us about our first day of school just this once.

I glance at Soap. Thank goodness she's wearing a nice shirt and corduroys. If only she'd lose ten pounds. Then she'd look perfect.

I feel queasy as we turn into the driveway of Miss Pringle's. Mrs. Sokoloff drops us off by the front porch. She pokes her head out of the window and says, "You know where you can reach me. 835 —"

"6700," finishes Soap.

"Good girl. I'll see you later. Ta-ta."

She waves her gloved hand and drives off. I'm glad to see her go.

There are a lot of girls on the porch. I quickly smooth my hair and pull up my knee socks. I hope I don't throw up.

"Are you nervous?" asks Soap.

"Just a little," I lie.

"Don't worry," says Soap. "I'll stick by you. Look. Here comes someone. She's probably supposed to show us around."

The girl coming toward us looks as if she's almost Jonah's age. She's tall, wears makeup, and has on a really pretty striped sweater.

"Hi," she says. "My name's Hilary Harwood. Mrs. Campbell, the eighth-grade homeroom teacher, asked me to show you where to go."

The bell rings, and we follow her into the school like two baby ducks following their mother.

"Did you come from Wood Valley?" she asks, as she leads us through a sun porch loaded with leafy plants and old-fashioned pillowy chairs.

"Yeah, but we got suspended for putting Saran Wrap over the toilets in the boys' john," says Soap.

"My goodness," says Hilary, raising one eyebrow. "That sounds like something my kid brother might do."

Darn Soap! Why can't she keep her mouth shut? We've only been here ten minutes, and already we've lost one potential friend.

The first grown-up I meet is our homeroom teacher, Mrs. Campbell. She has gray hair pulled back into a thin knot that's held together by one bobby pin. She's wearing orthopedic shoes and calls everyone Miss This and Miss That.

"This is Miss Endersby and Miss Sokoloff," she tells the class.

Then she asks Hilary to show us where to sit. Soap and I have to sit on opposite sides of the room. I guess Miss Pringle told Mrs. Campbell not to put us together. My desk is next to Hilary's.

I count fourteen girls besides Soap and me. Most of them are wearing clothes that look like they came from Belmont's, the most expensive store in Middletown.

The bell rings again and Mrs. Campbell tells us to line up for chapel. I can't believe it. In public school, we have to say the pledge of allegiance in homeroom, but at Miss Pringle's, we have to go to chapel.

It turns out that chapel means we go into this great big auditorium where we sing hymns and listen to Miss Pringle.

Suddenly my nose begins to itch, and I start to sneeze. Not just one big sneeze. I sneeze five times right in a row. "Ka-choo. Ka-choo. Ka-choo. Ka-choo. Ka-choo." It's awful. People turn and stare at me, and Soap starts to giggle. Luckily, the piano begins, and everyone bellows "God of Our Fathers, Whose Almighty Hand" at the top of their lungs. When we get to the last stanza, I sneeze again, and Mrs. Campbell glares at me. Soap is laughing hysterically, but I don't think it's funny.

I bump into everyone as I walk blindly out of chapel.

"Are you all right?" asks Soap.

"I guess so. I think I'm allergic to this place."

Soap giggles. "What's your first class?"

"Math."

"Good. Me, too."

Hilary comes over with another girl. "This is Julie French. She's going to take you to math class."

Hilary probably bribed Julie to look after us. Julie is wearing a madras skirt and an alligator shirt. She has a round, freckly face and blonde hair that bounces around her head.

Julie solemnly shakes both our hands. Good grief. Doesn't anyone in this school have a sense of humor?

"Come on," she says.

Mrs. Reynolds, the math teacher, is really

nice. The class is working on geometry, which we've never had, and she offers to tutor us each week until we catch up. Soap and I are going to be doing a lot of homework.

The rest of the morning goes quickly. We meet Mr. Bernstein, our history teacher, who's very dramatic. He bounces between his desk and the chairs while he makes a point. Sometimes he jumps right onto a chair and crouches on the seat, waving his arms around like some windmill.

Then we get to meet the English teacher, Miss Helms. She's tall and thin and has lots of bones that stick out — sharp shoulders, a sharp chin, and sharp elbows. She's very, very intelligent. She asks us to read aloud Act II of *A Midsummer Night's Dream*. I get the part of Puck, and she tells me that I've read it beautifully. I always knew I was good at dramatic reading, but I never had a chance to do it at Wood Valley. Of course, I turn bright red when she pays me the compliment.

Finally it's lunchtime. I'm famished. Soap and I stand in line and wait to have some greasy old ravioli dished out on oily-looking plates. The food at Miss Pringle's looks no better than the garbage we ate at Wood Valley.

"Shall we sit with Hilary and Julie?" I ask Soap.

"Are you kidding? After the way Hilary treated us this morning? Forget it. Let's sit alone."

I know how Soap feels, but I don't like being set apart as "a new girl." Only I can't tell this to Soap because she'd think it was stupid. We end up eating alone.

"What do you think of Mr. Bernstein?" I ask.

"He's okay. Even if he does hop around like a rabbit. But he sure did give us a big assignment. A whole chapter in that thick history book! When am I going to have time to do it? I want to watch TV tonight."

"Do it in study hall this afternoon," I say. "Period seven is free."

"But what about all the other homework?"

"I know. There's a ton of it. I don't see how we'll catch up in math. I didn't do that well in Mr. Krimsky's class, even when I *knew* what was going on."

"Don't worry," says Soap. "It's not *that* important. Many people have gotten through life only knowing how to add and subtract."

"Do you think Miss Helms will assign book reports?"

"Yeah, but you can write mine for me. You know how much I hate to write."

Julie and Hilary walk by without even glancing at us.

"They sure are stuck on themselves," says Soap when they're out of earshot. "I can't figure out why anyone would want to be friends with them."

I feel sort of irritated with Soap. I *do* want to be friends with them.

7. Eye Shadow

Soap sticks to me like chewing gum for the rest of the week. Once Julie comes over during lunch and I think she's going to ask to sit with us. But Hilary beckons her to another table, and again, Soap and I eat alone.

Sometimes I wish Soap wasn't with me so I'd *have* to make new friends. Every once in a while, I catch Hilary's eye, and I smile. Sometimes she smiles back for just an instant.

Then one day after gym class when we've just finished showers, I'm combing my wet hair, and Hilary is at the sink, putting on some eye makeup. She sees me watching her and she says, "Do you want to borrow some?"

"I've never tried it," I answer, and immediately want to kick myself.

"Really? Your eyes would look nice with a little shadow. Here, let me show you."

I look over my shoulder to see where Soap is, but she's nowhere around.

"Okay," I say.

I turn and face Hilary, then close my eyes. She's wearing perfume that reminds me of my grandmother's garden up in Maine. It's hard not to blink as Hilary rubs my eyelids.

"You're lucky. You have blue eyes. Everything goes with blue."

I can't help smiling at the compliment.

I wonder if her mother lets her wear makeup. I bet my mother wouldn't.

I wish Hilary'd hurry up. I'm dying to see how I look.

"Now open your eyes so that I can brush on some mascara."

I look up at the ceiling as Hilary coats my lashes. I try to keep my eyes from watering.

"There. Now you can look at yourself."

I turn and stare in the mirror. My eyes are shining like two stars.

"You *should* wear makeup. It makes your eyes look bluer."

The bell rings, and I feel all warm inside as I run to my locker.

Soap's leaning over in front of hers, tying the laces of her running shoes. I walk quickly by her and grab my books. Hilary comes up and takes my arm.

"Did you read that story by Stephen Spender?" she asks as she pulls me along to the door.

"Yep. But I didn't have a chance to —"

"Come on, Laurie." Soap shoves in front of Hilary and me and swings open the door.

"Excuse *me*!" remarks Hilary pointedly. Then she turns to me and says, "I guess you want to walk with *your friend*!"

She says "your friend" as if Soap were some piece of garbage. But I guess to Hilary she is. Soap doesn't pay much attention to her looks, and she's snubbed the other girls even more than they've snubbed her. Now she's gone and ruined everything, just when Hilary's started to be nice to me. I feel like hitting her.

"Let's all walk together," I murmur.

"No *way*," says Soap, as she pushes me toward the stairway to the next floor.

I look over my shoulder and see Hilary whispering something to Julie. They're probably talking about us. My face begins to burn and I turn around so I don't have to see them.

I walk down the corridor facing the wall so that Soap won't notice my eyes. But she already has.

"That eye goop looks disgusting," she says. "You look like you have two blue holes in your face."

I grab some Kleenex from my pocket and start wiping it off. It probably does look awful. I don't know why I let Hilary put it on me in the first place.

8. Belmont's Department Store

It's Saturday morning. I'm working on my English assignment. Miss Helms has asked us to write an autobiography. And she's given us only two weeks to do it. I've managed to squeeze out five lines so far:

I was born at 11:45 P.M., exactly, on New Year's Eve. As a result, my father says he got one year's income deduction. My mother was happy that I was a girl, since Jonah, her first child and my brother, had been a boy.

And now I'm stuck. Probably because hardly anything's happened to me in my thirteen years of life.

The phone rings. It's Soap. I'm no longer grounded.

"Do you want to do something?" she asks.

"Sure," I say. "Let's go to Belmont's. I need to buy a new blouse." I'm thinking about the white blouse Hilary was wearing on Friday. I want one just like it.

"You know I hate to go shopping," says Soap.

"Just for a few minutes?" I ask.

"Oh, all right. But then let's go to the movies. There's a neat old horror movie at the Gilbert."

I can't believe that Soap's actually agreed to go shopping with me.

We ride our bikes uptown and talk about Miss Pringle's.

"There's too much homework. And I don't like Hilary and Julie and the other clods they hang out with," says Soap.

"Maybe we haven't given them enough of a chance. After all, we've hardly talked to them. And I bet if we asked Julie to sit with us at lunch, she would."

Soap gives me a dirty look. "I think I'd throw up if I had to eat lunch with Julie."

Why does Soap have to be so negative?

When we get to Belmont's, we park our bikes and slide through the fancy doors that have brass handles on them in the shape of Bs. Mrs. Belmont is standing right smack in front of us when we walk in.

"Hello, dear," she says to me in her fudgy voice. "Is there anything I can help you with?"

My mother can't stand Mrs. Belmont. She always makes my mother try on clothes that look absolutely hideous on her. So my mother never shops there anymore. Actually, she never shops in stores, period. It makes her uncomfortable. Anything nice she has is stuff my father's bought her.

"We're going to look around," I say to Mrs. Belmont as I pull Soap toward the Clothespin, the boutique where the junior clothes are sold.

"Hurry up and get what you want," hisses Soap, "or Mrs. Belmont will make you try on every blouse in the store."

I go to the blouse rack, while Soap looks at T-shirts. I finally find the one I want. When I go to ask Soap her opinion, the saleslady tells me she's in the dressing room trying on a T-shirt. That's weird. Soap never tries on anything. I walk back and forth along the dressing-room corridors, poking my head between curtains, looking for Soap. Soap and I used to do this as kids, and sometimes we'd catch some lady naked from the waist up as she was trying on a bra. Soap's in the last booth.

"What do you think?" she asks.

She's wearing a navy blue T-shirt that's too small for her. She looks bulgy.

"It's too small. Why don't you try the next size?"

So while Soap gets another T-shirt, I try on the white blouse that's just like the one Hilary owns. It looks terrific with my jeans, and I like the little brown flowers that are embroidered around the neck. I decide to buy it.

I go look for the saleslady. Soap's waiting for me by the counter. She's cracking her knuckles.

"Did you find a T-shirt?" I ask.

"Nope," says Soap. "They're out of my size. Come on, Laurie, hurry up, or we'll be late for the movie."

I look at my watch. It's only one-thirty. The movie doesn't start for another half hour. Why is Soap so impatient?

"Okay, okay, I'm coming," I say as I pay the saleslady.

Mrs. Belmont smiles her lipsticky smile as we leave and says, "Give my best to your mothers. You might remind them that we have some darling pants on sale."

Then something terrible happens. As we push through the doors to the street, an alarm goes off. It sounds like a police siren. Soap turns pale as ice and starts running

down Main Street. I run after her, scream-
ing, "Soap, Soap, Soap," at the top of my
lungs. I can hear Mrs. Belmont running
behind me in her *clickety-clackety* high
heels. Soap grabs her bike and gasps, "I'll
be in the church." Then she pedals furi-
ously away. I can't figure out what's happened. I don't have time to, anyway,
because Mrs. Belmont screeches to a halt
beside me and starts firing questions. Her
makeup is swimming with sweat, and the
veins in her neck look like they're about to
burst.

"What did you girls steal? Come on, tell
me."

"Nothing," I answer.

"That alarm doesn't go off just to enter-
tain the customers. Come on, show me
what's in your bag."

So I show her the blouse and the sales
receipt. I'm beginning to feel like a crim-
inal. I'm convinced I've done something
wrong by the time Mrs. Belmont's exam-
ined the labels on practically everything
I'm wearing. Finally she seems satisfied
I'm not a thief.

"All right," she says. "Then it's that fat
friend of yours. That Sokoloff girl. She took
something. The alarm only goes off if the
security tag is still on merchandise leaving
the store."

"I'm sure Soap didn't take anything," I say. "I was with her the whole time, and I would have noticed."

"Did she try on anything?"

"Just a T-shirt," I say. "But you didn't have it in her size."

"Aha!" says Mrs. Belmont, licking her chops. "A T-shirt, huh? Well, I just happen to know that there was only one left in a size large. That fat friend of yours has gone off with it tucked beneath her parka. Wait till I tell Bernice Sokoloff about this!" And with that, Mrs. Belmont *clickety-clacks* back to the store.

Why would Soap steal a T-shirt? She doesn't even like T-shirts. And why did she have to go and mess up our afternoon? I *have* to find her.

I bicycle down Main Street as fast as I can and lean my bike against the hedge by the church walk. I let myself into the transept by a side door. The only light is filtering through the stained-glass windows, giving the empty church a lazy, whispery feeling.

"Soap? Are you here?" my voice booms.

"Shhhhh. Laurie, don't make so much noise," Soap whispers loudly. "I'm over here."

I can see her behind the baptismal font, crouched as if she's scared that Mrs. Belmont might be right behind me, ready to pounce on her. It would serve her right.

"Good grief, Soap. Mrs. Belmont is having kittens. She is really upset."

"She deserves it. I don't like her."

"But why'd you steal the T-shirt?"

"What do you mean, *why* did I steal the T-shirt? I wanted it, that's why."

"You're in for it now," I say. "Mrs. Belmont is going to call your mother."

"I don't care," says Soap, almost as if she *wants* her mother to find out.

She straightens up and heads for the aisle to the organ. "Come on, let's try 'Chopsticks.' "

I don't feel like it. I'm too nervous. Nervous that Mrs. Belmont might call the police. Nervous that Mr. Whitten might get angry if we play his organ. But most of all, I am furious at Soap, and I should let her know it.

She is slumped like some strange fish on the organ bench. "You play the bottom while I play the top," she says, beckoning to me.

I clench my teeth. I want to push her off that bench. Maybe she'll fall and hurt herself.

"Hurry up, Laurie." Her voice is teasing.

She flicks a switch, then pulls out some knobs.

I wish I could say something mean, but I can't. I'm just like Mom when Dad gets mad. I run away from anger, even my own.

I slowly climb the steps to the organ and sit down next to Soap. My hands feel heavy as I lift them to the keys and start to play.

Our duet sounds off-key as it drifts out over the pews. It makes me sick.

9. Hilary's House

When I get home, I am still feeling sick.
Mom tells me that Hilary has called and
asked me to spend the night. Of course, I
say yes, even though I'm a little nervous
about it. I've never slept over with anyone
but Soap.

I work for another hour or so on my
autobiography before I pack my bag and
bicycle over to Hilary's house.

Hilary's mother answers the door. She
looks like a slightly bigger version of Hilary, except she wears neat-looking glasses,
sort of smoky colored with thin, gold wire
frames.

"You must be Laurie," she says,, leading
me toward the kitchen. "Come meet Hilary's brother Fred, who's helping me cook
dinner. We're having filet mignon with
Béarnaise sauce. Hilary will be down in a

minute. She's talking long-distance to her father."

Boy, this sure isn't like Saturday night at our house — or any night, for that matter. Mom isn't much of a cook. If we're lucky, she'll make Swedish meatballs. Otherwise, it's hot dogs, hamburgers, or scrambled eggs. Sometimes Dad gets inspired and cooks a pepper steak, but only once in a blue moon.

Fred doesn't look anything like Hilary or her mother. He has bright red hair and freckled arms. He's standing over the stove, stirring some sauce.

"Hullo," he says.

Just then Hilary walks in. Her hair's soaking wet.

"Come on upstairs," she says, "while I dry my hair."

The walls of Hilary's room are covered with posters of rock and TV stars. She has a huge aquarium by her bed with at least fifteen fish in it.

"Where'd you get all the fish?" I ask.

"My dad gives me one every Christmas. He lives in California. The brightly colored ones with the spiny-looking fins are called butterfly fish."

"They're beautiful," I say. "My brother used to have an aquarium, but our dog knocked it over."

"Here, you can help me blow dry my hair," says Hilary, as she hands me the dryer. "We'll do it in my mother's room."

Hilary sits down at her mother's dressing table. Its glass top looks like a photograph album. Pictures of Fred, Hilary, and what must be various relatives are held down in neat rows beneath the glass. One of the pictures is of Hilary's mother and a tall, red-haired man with freckles and a painful-looking sunburn. He looks very nice. He's wearing a bathing suit and has his arm around Hilary's mother. I figure that he must be Hilary's father.

I'm standing there holding the hair dryer. Good grief. This is embarrassing. First I had to admit I'd never worn makeup. Now I have to admit I don't know how to use a hair dryer. Hilary will send me downstairs to play with Fred.

I brush Hilary's dripping hair over her face. Then I flick the switch of the hair dryer to ON and wave it back and forth across the hair.

"Ouch," says Hilary. "What are you doing? You're blowing hot air right into my face! Haven't you ever done this before?"

I look down at my feet. I can feel my face getting hot.

"Un-unh."

"Why didn't you say so? It's easy. All you do is clip my hair up into layers. Then you take the brush, fold a layer around it, and dry it."

"Okay. I'll try."

"Hey, have you ever cut your hair?"

"It's been trimmed lots of times, but it's been long ever since I was a kid."

Suddenly Hilary's whole face changes. It's as if a light switch goes on inside her head.

"Come on," she says.

She grabs my arm and yanks me toward the bathroom. What is her problem?

"Sit down on the toilet seat," she commands. Then she ties a towel around my neck. Naturally, it has a monogram on it. So does the toilet-seat cover and the bath mat and shower curtain. Next she opens the medicine cabinet and pulls out a pair of cutting shears.

"I'm going to cut your hair," she says. "It will look terrific short."

Oh, no, she's serious! How can I trust my hair to practically a total stranger? My long, silky hair.

"Please don't cut it," I say. "I . . . I like it long."

"Don't be silly. You'll look much better with it short."

"But . . . what if I look awful with short hair?"

"You won't. Trust me."

"All right," I say weakly.

Hilary starts cutting, and my blonde locks fall in scraps to the spotless tile floor. The tears well up in my eyes. I look down so Hilary can't see.

"What kind of shampoo do you use?" Hilary asks.

"Johnson's baby shampoo," I answer, my voice trembling.

"Your hair seems dry. You should use a rinse — I'll lend you some of my mother's. It will make your hair shinier."

As Hilary snips away, she asks, "Is Soap your best friend?"

I hesitate for a second before saying, "Yes."

"What's she like?"

Even though I'm angry at Soap, I know it's only temporary. I want Hilary to like her. It would be nice if we could all be friends.

"She's crazy and fun. She loves to do stuff that makes people mad. If it wasn't for her, I wouldn't have come to Miss Pringle's."

"What do you mean?"

"Her parents thought she'd get into less trouble if she went to a different school.

See, she used to do a lot of wild things, be-sides just putting Saran Wrap on toilet seats."

"What else did she do?"

"One time she let the air out of the tires of the cars in the faculty parking lot. She never got caught for that, luckily. And she used to hide alarm clocks in the French room, and they'd go off halfway through class. She did lots of stuff."

As I'm talking, I find that I'm sort of proud of Soap's stunts. You have to give her credit for being imaginative. But Hilary doesn't see it that way.

"That's the kind of stuff Fred and his friends do. And Fred's only in fourth grade."

I guess she's right. I wish she would stop cutting. Finally, when I start squirming, she's done.

"There!" she says.

I'm scared to look in the mirror. I know I'll look like a plucked chicken.

Actually, I don't look that bad. In fact, I look pretty neat. Certainly older.

"I'm not through," says Hilary. "You have to wet your hair now. Then I can get the sides to be exactly even."

By the time she's finished and my hair's blown dry, I look almost ravishing. Like some TV star.

Hilary's mother likes it. "It makes you look older," she says, as we eat our filet mignon with Béarnaise sauce. "You should have done it ages ago. Just think of all the fun you've missed."

This doesn't quite make sense to me. I mean, basically a person should have fun or not have fun regardless of his or her hairstyle. Maybe Hilary's mother is one of those people who changes her hairstyle every time she's bored.

"I don't like girls with short hair," says Fred, as he grabs a roll in each hand. "I don't think it's feminine."

"Honestly," says Hilary, "you don't know anything."

After we finish dinner and clear the table, we go upstairs to Hilary's room.

"I'll try on my new nightie," Hilary says as she goes over to her closet. She slips off her clothes and pulls on a black nylon gown with spaghetti straps. It gives her lots of cleavage.

I look down at my own flat chest and think about the red flannel pajamas I've packed in my overnight bag. I feel sort of stupid. Hilary is so much more . . . more sophisticated.

"Do you want to watch TV? There's a movie on tonight called *Forever*. It's based on a book by Judy Blume."

"Sure."

"You change while I go downstairs and get some cookies and Coke."

"Okay."

I don't want to undress in front of Hilary, so I wait until she leaves. Then I lock myself in the bathroom and put on my pajamas. They look baggy, and I feel bony and lost in them as I look in the mirror. My new hair doesn't go with them. I think back to how happy I was when I first tried them on at Christmas last year.

As I walk into the bedroom, Hilary's fiddling with the dial on her color TV set. She's put the snacks on the table between our beds. I wish I had a TV set in my room! Hilary looks at my pajamas and blanches.

"Try on the other nightgown I bought this afternoon. It's just like the one I'm wearing, only it's pink."

Before I can even answer, Hilary waltzes over to the bureau and pulls out a filmy garment. It glows mysteriously in the light from the TV screen.

I take it and retreat to the bathroom. I pull off my pajamas and yank the pink gown over my head and shoulders. Then I stare at myself in the mirror. It's cut much too low for my flat chest, but even so, it makes me look different. Older. My waist is smaller than my hips, and my shoulders look wider.

I feel giddy as I step out of the bathroom. Hilary is sitting up in bed, rubbing cream under her eyes.

"That's much better," she says. "You look good in pink. It goes with your blue eyes and blonde hair." She yawns. "The program's starting. The bed near the door is yours."

The movie is really good. It's about a girl whose feelings for her old boyfriend change after she falls in love with a counselor at summer camp.

Hilary asks during a commercial, "Do you have a boyfriend?"

Now she'll find out how really backward I am. Another reason for her to think I'm dumb.

"No," I mumble.

"Don't you ever go on dates?" she asks.

"No one's ever asked me to. . . . Do you?"

"Oh, lots of times," she says, as if she's talking about how often she brushes her teeth. "Tonight, in fact, I was supposed to go to the movies with Boots Bailey, but he backed out because his parents came to visit. He goes to Middletown Prep."

"I've never met anyone from there," I say, "but I used to bicycle past it on my way to Wood Valley. It's a boys' boarding school, right?"

"Right," answers Hilary. "Anyway, I'm giving a party next Saturday night. Do you want to come? I want you to meet Boots' roommate, Sam Fraker, and several other guys from Middletown. They're all sophomores. I'm only going to ask you and Julie and Stacy and Phoebe."

I feel flattered. And scared. What will I say to Boots' friend? Even with Jonah's friends, I get tongue-tied. And how about Soap? Won't she be disgusted that I'm going to a party at Hilary's? I want to go, and I don't want to go.

As I nuzzle my face into the soft, smooth, monogrammed sheets, I think about the problems of having a new friend.

10. Mr. Sokoloff's Secret

When I get home from Hilary's on Sunday, Mom's sitting at the dining-room table doing *The New York Times* crossword puzzle. She takes one look at me and says, "Pumpkin, what on earth did you do to your hair?"

"Hilary cut it. Do you like it?"

"Well," says Mom, "I don't know. You certainly look different. More ... grown-up. It looks ... nice. It just takes some getting used to. Why'd you do it?"

"It just sort of happened," I say. "We were fooling around with Hilary's hair dryer, and before I knew it, my hair was lying on the floor."

Just then Dad walks in. He's wearing his tennis clothes.

"Hi," he says, as he walks toward the kitchen to get to the garage, where the car's parked.

"Bob!" says Mom, "look at your daughter!"

Dad looks, and his jaw drops about a hundred feet.

"Laurie! You cut your hair!"

"That's right, Dad. You're looking at the new me."

"Mmmmmmm," says Dad.

"Don't you like it?"

"I guess so. It's just that. . . . Well, I'm going to miss your long hair."

Typical. Why can't my parents get used to the fact that I'm thirteen years old?

I practice awhile on the piano, then go upstairs to do some more work on my autobiography.

The first thing I remember as a little kid is the time I got pneumonia. I had to go to the hospital, where I was put in an oxygen tent. It was like being inside of a big cellophane bag. My parents used to visit me every day. Sometimes they would bring me strawberries. The nurse would poke them through a hole that she unzipped in the tent.

It's painful to remember being in the hospital. The nurses used to wake me up at all hours of the night and take my blood.

And always I was coughing, coughing, coughing. Just as I'm about to write about the coughing part, the phone rings. It's Soap.

"Do you want to come over?" she asks.

I really don't want to see Soap that much. I'm still mad at her, and besides, I am really getting somewhere on my autobiography. So I say, "I just got home from spending the night at Hilary's, and I want to do some homework. Maybe I can come over another time."

"Are you *still* working on that stupid autobiography?"

Knowing Soap, she probably hasn't even started hers.

"I think it's kind of fun to remember the stuff that happened a long time ago," I say.

"How many funny things can happen in only thirteen years of life?"

"Lots of things. Like getting caught smoking, getting suspended from school for putting Saran Wrap over the boys' room toilets —"

"— and being with your best friend when she steals a T-shirt," finishes Soap with a nasty little laugh.

"Did you get in trouble?" I ask.

"Not really. My mother gave me a lecture, but that's all. And you know my father. He's always in some other world."

Sometimes I wonder why Soap's parents bothered to have her.

There's a pause. Then Soap says, "So you spent the night at Hilary's, huh?" She sounds jealous. "What were you doing there?"

"You'll see," I say. "I have a surprise."

"Oh, come on, Laurie. Tell me!"

"Nope. I'll have to *show* you."

"Then you *have* to come over!"

I can just picture Soap's face when she sees my hair. She'll like it, I bet.

"Okay. I'll be there around three o'clock," I say.

When I get to her house, Mr. Sokoloff answers the door.

"How're you doing, Laurie?" he asks.

"Okay," I say. "How's your article on termites going?"

"I finished it," he says. "Now I'm doing research on praying mantises. I think Soap's in the kitchen making a batik."

I just figured out why Soap's father likes insects so much. He looks sort of like a praying mantis.

"Laurie!" yells Soap. "Come help me. Quick! There's a hole in the dye bucket."

I dash into the kitchen, and the floor is a mess. Blue dye is spilling down the edge of the table. Soap is trying to lift the bucket of dye over to the sink. I grab hold of the other side, and we carry it across the room, leaving a trail of blue water behind us.

"Here, take these towels and start mopping," orders Soap.

As I soak up the dye on the floor and table, Soap lifts some cloth from the bucket and carries it to a clothesline at the other end of the kitchen. She leaves a trail of blue dye behind her. I get some more towels and mop up the mess as best I can.

After Soap pins up the dripping blue cloth, she turns to me and gasps, "Laurie, what have you done to your hair?"

"I cut it," I say. "Actually, Hilary cut it. Do you like it?"

"No," says Soap. "It makes you look like a cabbage. Why'd you let *her* do it?"

I should have known Soap would be mean. Just like she was when I wore eye shadow. I feel like throwing the wet towels at her, but I'm too chicken, as usual. Instead, I say, "I thought I'd look better with short hair."

Just then Mrs. Sokoloff comes into the kitchen.

"Girls! What on earth have you been doing? This place is disgusting, and I have to cook for a dinner party tonight."

"Don't get hysterical," says Soap. "I've

been making a batik. But I'll wait and finish it next weekend."

"You should have asked me about using the kitchen," says Mrs. Sokoloff.

"You were upstairs on the phone, and besides, Pops said it would be okay," says Soap.

"He would!" says Mrs. Sokoloff. "He has no idea how messy batik-making is."

"Let's beat a hasty retreat," says Soap under her breath.

I wonder who's going to mop up the rest of the kitchen. But I find out soon enough.

"Irrrrrving," calls Mrs. Sokoloff. "Could you come here?"

Now if my parents had found out I had made a mess, I would have had to clean it up myself.

Soap grabs my arm, and we run up the back stairs to her room.

"My mother never lets me do anything fun," complains Soap.

She walks back and forth in front of her desk, then sits down on the bed. "What do you feel like doing?"

"I dunno."

Soap fiddles with the ears on her Snoopy dog — one of the many stuffed animals she keeps on her bed. She's really getting too old to have stuffed animals. Hilary doesn't have any in her room, and I put mine away last summer.

"I know." Soap's face lights up. "Let's play some telephone jokes on our teachers. Don't you think Mrs. Campbell would die if we told her she had been selected out of a sampling of five hundred women to get a free face-lift?"

Soap starts to giggle. But I don't feel like it. I'm just not in the mood to play a bunch of silly telephone jokes. It seems so immature.

"Come on," says Soap. "Mom is busy cooking, so she won't even know that we're using the phone."

She drags me into her parents' bedroom, where she picks up the phone book. She looks up Mrs. Campbell's number and is just about to dial when she gets this worried look on her face. She puts her hand over the receiver.

"Pops is on the phone downstairs in the den, and . . . he's talking to some woman!"

Soap's face changes from curiosity to disgust to joy.

"Oh, brother," she whispers. "I think Pops has a girl friend. I just heard him say that he couldn't wait to see this person again — he called her darling — and told her that he loved her!"

I'm shocked. The thought of Mr. Sokoloff

being with anyone but Mrs. Sokoloff is very, very strange.

"Are you sure it was your father's voice?" I ask.

"Of course I'm sure," says Soap. "Anyway, who else could it have been?"

Neither of us says anything.

Finally I say, "I'm sure you heard wrong. Anyhow, you only heard a part of his conversation. He could have been rehearsing lines for some play or something."

"Sure," says Soap, "a play. Pops has never been in a play in his life. And why would anyone rehearse into a phone? Hey, I think it's neat he has a girl friend. I just hope my mother doesn't find out."

I can't believe my ears.

"Aren't you upset?" I ask.

"Why should I be?" she answers. "My mother is a witch, and it serves her right!"

"Soap!" How can she say that? Even if it's true.

"We have to find out more about it," says Soap.

There's that "we" again. But I don't want to know more about it. I think parents should stick together, not cheat behind each other's backs. Otherwise, how can they trust one another?

"We can listen in on the phone. Check out Pops' wallet and clothes and stuff for clues. . . . Hey, you know what? That woman's voice sounded sort of familiar. Like maybe I've met her somewhere before."

I feel very uncomfortable. I wish I was home right now. "Don't be ridiculous. Your father wouldn't be dumb enough to have an affair with someone in Middletown. It's too small."

"You're probably right," says Soap. "But let's look in Pops' desk before he comes upstairs. You keep guard while I go through his papers."

Soap runs out of the bedroom and down the hall to his office. But I don't follow her. It's none of my business. And besides, what if we got caught?

She sticks her head around the corner of the door.

"What are you waiting for? We have to *hurry*. Pops might come upstairs any minute."

I want to run away, but I can't. Soap's presented me with another irresistible situation. If I leave now, I'll never find out about Mr. Sokoloff's mystery woman. Maybe she's some actress. Or some famous scientist. I know I shouldn't stay and spy; it's not right, but. . . .

Soap sticks her head around the corner again.

"I think I've found another clue," she says. "There's a tube of lipstick in Pops' briefcase."

That does it.

I hold my breath as I follow Soap down the hall.

"It's burnt beige. That's how I know it's not my mother's. She always wears red."

Soap shuffles through some of Mr. Sokoloff's papers, while I stand panic-stricken by the door. She doesn't find anything else, thank goodness.

"I've got to go," I say.

"Okay," says Soap. "I'll call you later if I find out anything else."

"All right," I answer. But a voice inside of me says, "You don't want to know. It can only mean trouble."

I look at Mrs. Sokoloff's stiff back as I walk by her in the kitchen. If she even suspected her husband was having an affair, I bet she'd treat him differently. Not boss him around so much. Maybe it wouldn't be bad if she found out. Maybe it would make her love her family more.

11. More Clues

In school Monday morning, there's a verse scrawled on the blackboard in homeroom. It's a limerick, which isn't surprising, since we've been learning about limericks in Miss Helms' English class.

Miss Pringle's girls are icky,
Ridiculous and yicky.
A bunch of snobs,
And sickly slobs,
They all act very cliqu-ey.

Mrs. Campbell is furious. Of course, I know who did it. Soap. So that's why she didn't ride her bicycle to school with me this morning.

"We're going to sit here," says Mrs. Campbell, "until one of you admits to having done this."

Hilary whispers something to Julie, and

they both look at Soap. In fact, everyone's looking at her. But she's looking out the window with a smirk on her face. Typical.

After ten minutes of uncomfortable silence, Mrs. Campbell says, "I'm very disappointed that the culprit didn't feel moved to confess, so I'm going to keep the whole class after school for an extra hour."

Everyone starts to murmur in protest. Soap sure knows how to make enemies. Why does she have to act so stupid? It makes me feel disloyal. I wish she cared more about school and grades. Like Hilary.

As Hilary and I walk to her house Thursday afternoon, she asks me how I'm doing on my autobiography.

"I'm almost done," I say. "How about you?"

"Only one chapter to go," she answers. "I want the last chapter to be about my plans and ambitions."

"What do you mean?" I ask.

"I'd like to be a famous writer of savage romances."

I've heard about "savage romances," but I don't know what they are. Hilary explains that they're romances that take place in the past and that they have a lot of sex and passion.

"I've been thinking," she continues,

"about our history project for Mr. Bernstein. I have a good idea, but I need your help. My mother has been taking a course in women's studies, and she's been reading a lot about famous women in history. They're not mentioned very often in our history books, but more and more is being written about them. For example, did you know that a woman ran for President in 1872? Her name was Victoria Woodhull, and a lot of people thought she was crazy because she believed in free love."

"You're kidding!" I can't wait to hear more.

"And there was also a famous woman named Susan B. Anthony who did more than any other woman to get women the right to vote. There's even a dollar coin that has her head on it."

"Good grief," I say. "I haven't read about any of these women."

"That's the point," says Hilary. "That's why I think they'd be good subjects for a history project. They're in hardly any textbooks. I could report on Victoria Woodhull, and you could do Susan B. Anthony. There's also a woman named Elizabeth Cady Stanton who worked closely with Susan B. Anthony. Maybe we could get someone else to do a report on her."

"How about Soap?" I say.

"This is a *serious* project," says Hilary. "Soap would just goof off and ruin everything."

"No, she wouldn't," I say. "She works hard when she's interested in something."

I have to stick up for her. I have to make Hilary see her good side. I'm tired of being pulled in two.

"But Laurie, she's gotten nothing but Ds and Fs since she's been at Miss Pringle's. Anyway, I don't really want to work with anyone but you. We don't have to have a third person. We can do Elizabeth Cady Stanton ourselves. We can work together every afternoon. Just you and me and no one else."

Suddenly I don't feel like I'm being pulled in two anymore. I'm on Hilary's side. Soap is going to have to learn to fend for herself. I'm not going to let her ruin my friendship with Hilary.

When I get home, Mom tells me that Jonah is coming home for Thanksgiving. Before he went to college, I couldn't wait to get rid of him. But now that he's been gone, I've missed him. I'm looking forward to seeing him again. And Thanksgiving is only a week away. Maybe Hilary would like to meet him.

As I'm looking up Susan B. Anthony in our *Encyclopaedia Britannica*, Soap calls.

"I found out more about her," she says. Her voice sounds really excited.

"Who?" I ask.

"Don't you remember?" She sounds impatient. "Pops' girl friend. She lives in Middletown."

"Oh." I try not to sound too interested. But my curiosity is aroused. Who in Middletown could possibly be in love with Mr. Sokoloff?

"I listened in on another phone conversation," Soap continues. "And guess what? Pops is going to meet her tomorrow at twelve-thirty. They don't want anyone to see them together, so they're meeting during lunch at the World War II monument in Rayburn Park. She kept telling him how worried she was that she'd bump into someone she knew. He kept telling her it wouldn't matter — that no one would suspect anything even if the two of them *were* seen together."

Now I'm *dying* of curiosity.

"Who do you think she is?"

"I don't know, but I'm planning to find out. I think we should spy on them tomorrow."

"But Soap, we can't. We'll be in school. Besides, what if your father sees us?"

"I've got it all figured out," says Soap. "We can park our bikes tomorrow morning by the church. Then, at lunch, we can sneak out the door by the gym, walk behind the bushes that go to the property next door, cross the street, pick up our bikes, and ride over to the park. It's only a mile away. We can leave our bikes in the woods and hide near the monument."

"But what if we don't get back in time for math class? We could get suspended."

I'm also worried about how Hilary might react. If we got caught, it would finish things between us.

"There's no way things can go wrong. I've thought of everything. Look, we'll tell Julie that I'm taking you to the nurse because of a stomachache. Then, if we're not back by sixth period, she'll tell Mrs. Reynolds we're still at the nurse's. I'm sure Mrs. Reynolds won't check. Anyway, we'll leave the park in time to get back for math class. There's nothing that can go wrong."

But I'm not so sure. In the past when things *couldn't* go wrong, they always did. I don't want to take any more risks.

"I can't do it. It's too dangerous. Lots of things could happen to screw things up. I don't want to get into trouble."

"Honestly, Laurie, you're turning into a regular party pooper. All you want to do is study, study, study. And hang around with Hilary. If you're not careful, you'll get stuck up. Just like her." She pauses for a second. "Don't you realize how *important* this is? It's the most important thing in my whole life. You *have* to do it. For me. As my *best* friend. As my *oldest* friend. As the *only* person in the world I can trust."

Soap's words slice into me. ". . . you'll get stuck up. Just like her." Isn't that something I want to avoid? It's what I hated about Miss Pringle's girls before I came. I feel confused. I thought I wanted to push Soap away so she wouldn't hurt my chances of having some new friends. But now I'm not so sure. She sounds so desperate. And this is different from anything she's asked me to do before. She really needs me.

"Okay," I say. "I'll meet you tomorrow morning so we can park our bikes at the church."

"I knew you'd do it," says Soap. "You won't regret it."

12. Rayburn Park Disaster

Leaving during lunch hour turns out to be more difficult than we thought. Mr. Bernstein asks Soap to stay after class to tell him why she hasn't found a subject for her nineteenth-century America report. And Julie and Hilary ask me to sit with them during lunch to talk about Hilary's party.

"I'll be late," I murmur. "Soap's taking me to the nurse. I have a stomachache. If we don't show up at math class, could you tell Mrs. Reynolds where we are?"

I clutch at my stomach so as to be convincing.

"See you later," says Hilary. She doesn't sound as friendly as usual. Probably because I asked Soap to take me to the nurse instead of her.

It seems like Mr. Bernstein keeps Soap for hours. I wait for her on the window seat in the hall outside of the classroom. Finally she comes out.

"I had to tell him that I had a headache. Otherwise he would have kept me right through lunch. And all because I didn't do my dumb homework."

"We'd better hurry," I say. "I feel like bugs are crawling around inside me. Now I do have a stomachache."

Our getaway goes all right. As far as I can tell, no one sees us leave, and we get to the park by quarter after twelve.

There are a few people with children in the park playground, but no one's near the path to the monument in the woods.

We park our bikes behind some rhododendron bushes.

"I know," says Soap. "Let's climb that oak tree. Then we'll be able to hear everything."

I haven't climbed a tree since I was five years old, and I'm not sure it's worth it. But I scramble up into the branches like some monkey. As usual, I'm a lot more nervous than Soap. I can't figure her out. If I was about to see my father's mistress, I think my heart would be skipping beats by now. But Soap is sitting calmly on the branch above me.

"I think I hear someone coming," she whispers.

Sure enough. There's the sound of shoes on the gravel path.

It's Mr. Sokoloff. He looks like he's been through a car wash. His hair is wetted down neatly, and his skin has been scrubbed apple-skin shiny. He's wearing a nice trench coat and green corduroy pants. He's carrying a paper bag, and he keeps looking at his watch.

Then we see her.

She's wearing dark glasses and keeps looking around as she crosses the baseball diamond near the path to the monument. There's something familiar about the way she's moving. That long, tall body with the bony shoulders and elbows. That big chin.

Good grief. It's Miss Helms!

"Oh, no," says Soap under her breath.

"Shhhhh," I say.

I'd give anything to be eating lunch with Hilary and Julie right now. This is too much.

When Miss Helms gets to the monument, she looks around again and then gives Mr. Sokoloff a quick, bony hug. This could get really embarrassing!

They sit down with their sharp shoulders touching.

"I wasn't able to do a jot of work all morning. Every time I tried to concentrate,

79.

I started thinking about you," says Mr. Sokoloff.

He gives her a big, slurpy kiss. Right on the lips.

"Me, too," says Miss Helms. "About you."

They kind of sit and stare at each other for a minute.

Then Mr. Sokoloff says, "When do you have to go back?"

"In time for my next class. I can stay for only half an hour."

"I wish you could stay all afternoon."

"Me, too," says Miss Helms.

There's this big silence while they stare at each other again.

Then she says, "It's frustrating to see you so little."

"I know," says Mr. Sokoloff. "I've been thinking a lot about it."

"Irving, you're going to have to make up your mind. It's dangerous to go on like this."

"I know."

"And I hate seeing Lucinda every day in class. It makes me feel . . . guilty!"

I look up at Soap. She's leaning way down so as to hear every word. She looks grim. I try to guess what's going through her head. Is she wondering if her parents are going to split up? Is she shocked that

Miss Helms is her father's girl friend? Is she thinking about how they met? And how long it's been going on?

"Wouldn't you feel just as guilty if she did know?" asks Mr. Sokoloff.

"I guess I would. But at least we wouldn't be sneaking around like two criminals."

Mr. Sokoloff kisses Miss Helms gently on the forehead.

"I know we can't go on like this. I'll tell Bernice soon."

"Good."

"I brought you some lunch," says Mr. Sokoloff. "A mustard sandwich!"

"Mustard?"

"It's all I could find in the refrigerator."

"I'll eat anything at this point. I'm famished."

Soap's father hands Miss Helms her sandwich and then bites into his own. They both start eating like two starving animals.

"How's your article going?" asks Miss Helms.

"I'm almost finished. I have to fly up to Boston during Thanksgiving weekend to verify one piece of research. There's a professor there I need to interview. He's the world's leading authority on praying mantis eggs."

"You are interested in the most amazing things!"

"Yes," says Mr. Sokoloff. "Are you still planning to visit your family in Auburn for Thanksgiving? Because I was thinking it would be fun to meet in Boston. We could go to the aquarium, and walk along the Charles, and go to the science museum, and —"

"I'd love to!" says Miss Helms and throws her arms around Soap's father. She practically knocks him over. She's almost as enthusiastic about Soap's father as she is about Shakespeare. Maybe even more so.

"Guess what I'm doing my next article on."

"What?"

"Tarantulas. Did you know that thirty species live in the United States? They live in burrows and come out at night to hunt. Some tropical species prey on birds and can kill and eat small poisonous snakes. . . ."

It's strange to hear Mr. Sokoloff talk so much after seeing him around Soap's mother. Miss Helms looks like she's actually interested in what he's saying. But after a while she cuts him off.

"Irving . . . how do you think Lucinda will feel? If you leave Bernice, I mean?"

"She'll be able to handle it. I've read that kids aren't nearly as upset by their parents breaking up as some people think."

I look up at Soap. Her mouth is trembling. I can't tell if it's because she's angry or because she's about to cry. Her knuckles are white and pinched as she clutches the tree limb she's sitting on. She turns her head so I can't see her face. Or maybe it's so she won't have to see any more of the scene below. So her father's affair *is* beginning to get to her.

I look down again. Miss Helms and Mr. Sokoloff are kissing. Finally, after what seems like hours, they pull away. Miss Helms' burnt beige lipstick is all over Mr. Sokoloff's face. Oh, brother.

"I'll call you tonight," says Mr. Sokoloff.

Miss Helms dabs at his face with a Kleenex.

"I'm stopping at the Y after school. But I'll be home by six."

"Good."

After they leave, Soap climbs down from the tree without saying anything. She picks up her bike and starts wheeling it along the path. It looks like she's struggling hard not to cry. I wheel my bike up next to her. I want to reach out, but it's hard to know how. I've never seen her like this.

"It was harder than you expected, huh?"

The tears start to roll down her face. "Yes," she sniffles. "Especially since it's

Miss Helms. How could they do this to me? I feel so . . . so left out. As if they're waging some secret war against me."

"But Soap, they're not seeing each other because they want to be mean to you. It's because they love each other."

"But I want them to love me, too."

"They do love you. They just can't show it because their relationship is a secret."

"If they loved me, they'd care more about how this whole thing makes *me* feel. Sometimes I think the entire world hates me." Soap starts to cry harder.

"*I* don't hate you," I say.

"Sometimes I think you do. Especially now that you're going around with Hilary."

I feel caught in the middle. Again.

"My whole life is falling apart," Soap continues, between sobs, "and you're the only person I can turn to."

I wish she hadn't said that. I feel closer to her, but I also feel responsible for her. As if she'd go to pieces if I deserted her.

"Come on, Soap. You're still my best friend. Now here, blow your nose. Sixth period starts in ten minutes. We have to leave right now, or we'll be really, really late."

"Will you promise not to tell anyone about what happened?" she asks.

"I promise," I say. "Now, will you be all right if we go back to school?"

"Yeah, I'll be all right."

Only she's not. We don't make it in time, and Mrs. Reynolds has gone to tell Miss Pringle that we've disappeared.

13. More Trouble

"Where were you?" hisses Hilary after we walk into math class. "Mrs. Reynolds sent Stacy to the nurse's to see if you were okay, and the nurse said you had never been there. Mrs. Reynolds has gone to Miss Pringle's office."

Good grief. Things are getting hairy. Just what I was afraid of.

"Where were you?" Hilary asks again. Soon everyone's standing around us, waiting for an answer.

"It's none of your business," says Soap sourly and flops down at a desk.

"Well, you don't have to be so snippy about it," says Hilary.

Just then Mrs. Reynolds appears at the door.

"I see you've returned," she says coldly. "You're wanted in Miss Pringle's office."

Everyone's staring at us. I'm scared. I

look away, but Soap gets up and marches past Mrs. Reynolds and out the door. I follow her to Miss Pringle's office.

Miss Pringle greets us curtly and motions us to sit down. She arranges herself neatly in the chair behind her desk and says, "I'd like you to explain to me where you were during lunch."

I have to think of something fast. I'm used to Soap's doing the talking for both of us, but this time I have to play her role.

"Uptown," I say quickly. "At the . . . the Sunshine Pizzeria."

"I'm very disappointed in both of you," says Miss Pringle. "You know it's against the rules to leave school property without permission."

"I'm sorry," I say. "I know we shouldn't have. It's just that we were tired of eating in the cafeteria."

"Everyone gets tired of eating in the same place every day. What makes you so different from everyone else? The other students obey the rule."

"I'm sorry," I mumble again, looking at my feet.

"And you, Lucinda?"

"I'm sorry, too," says Soap. She sounds it, although I know it's because of her father, not because of Miss Pringle.

"You'll get only a warning this time.

But if you break one more rule, I'll call a special meeting of the faculty. Our school prides itself on good citizenship. We don't tolerate exhibitions of irresponsibility. You can go back to class now."

My face is bright red as we enter Mrs. Reynolds' room.

I hate Soap for making me suffer like this. I stare at some figures on the blackboard to avoid Hilary's scornful eyes. I'm sure that now she won't want me at her party.

But she does. She calls me later to remind me that it's tomorrow night and invites me to stay over afterwards.

Before she hangs up, she asks me the question I've been dreading.

"Why won't you tell me where you went with Soap?"

"I . . . I promised her. . . ."

"I won't tell anyone."

I wish she wouldn't press me. It makes it hard not to tell.

"I bet you were helping Soap with one of her childish tricks."

"No, no . . . it wasn't anything like that. We were at . . . at the Sunshine Pizzeria."

"Sure. You biked three miles over and three miles back, just for one dumb pizza. Come on, Laurie, where'd you really go?"

Thank goodness Mom calls me just then.

"Laurie, would you please set the table for dinner?"

"I have to go," I say hurriedly. "Mom needs me in the kitchen."

I hang up the phone before Hilary can answer.

Good old Mom. By tomorrow, Hilary will have forgotten all about it. She'll be too busy thinking about her party.

14. Hilary's Party

Before the party, I wash my hair. I borrow Mom's hair dryer because I want my hair to look as nice as it did the day Hilary cut it.

Mom comes into my room just as I'm finishing.

"Do you need help?" she asks.

"No, thanks. I'm almost done. Do I look all right?" I'm wearing my new blouse from Belmont's with jeans.

"You look very pretty," says Mom, "although I miss your long hair. Anyway, you shouldn't worry so much."

Typical Mom.

"Don't you ever get nervous before you go to a party?" I ask.

"I used to," says Mom. "But I learned a trick. When I feel that way, I start thinking that other people must be feeling just as shy and frightened as I am. It helps."

Hmmmm. Maybe I'll try that.

Mom drives me to Hilary's house. The windows are open, as usual.

"My hair's getting ruined!" I say as I roll up my window.

"Sorry." Mom slows down.

Napoleon sits in the backseat and leans over my shoulder. He drools down my neck.

"Quit it!" I push him away.

I am really glad when we get there.

Hilary answers the door in pink satin jeans and a sparkly red top. There's something different about her. I can't figure out what it is until she says, "My mother let me use some of her new makeup." That's it. Instead of wearing blue eye shadow, she's painted her eyelids brown, and she's wearing brownish lipstick.

"Come on upstairs," she says. "Try Mom's new makeup, the sultry look."

I don't know if I want to look sultry. But I let her put it on me. When she's through, I don't look like Laurie anymore. I look like Hilary, only with blonde hair. It feels weird, as if I'm in someone else's body.

The doorbell rings, and it's Julie. She's wearing a blue jean skirt and clogs, and her hair's bouncier than ever.

Hilary's mother comes down the front hall.

"Fred and I are going to start heating up the coq au vin," she says to Hilary.

"Wait a while, Mom, all right? Boots isn't even here yet. Let's wait at least an hour before bringing out dinner. And please don't spy on us every two seconds."

"Of course not," says Hilary's mother. "Fred and I are going to play gin rummy in the kitchen."

Just then the doorbell rings again. My hands are clammy, and the eye shadow itches my eyelids. Why can't I be as relaxed as Hilary and Julie? I wish I were with Soap.

"Hi, Boots," says Hilary. "You already know Julie. This is Laurie."

Boots looks like he's from California — all blond and smiley and healthy. He bounds over to me and sticks out his hand. "Hello, hello, hello," he shouts enthusiastically.

I can't help but step back.

"Hi," I murmur, letting him pump my hand up and down.

Three more boys walk in behind him. "This is my roommate, Sam Fraker," says Boots. "And Dick and Rick, who live down the hall from us."

Good grief. Dick and Rick? What kind of weird names are those? Sam Fraker is tall with short brown hair and loafers. He looks like an ad for *The Official Preppy Handbook*.

I manage to say hello, but I feel scared inside. And nervous. Maybe if I comb my hair and put on some more of Hilary's mother's makeup, I'll feel better.

When no one's looking, I dash upstairs to the bathroom. I peer at myself in the mirror. My hair doesn't seem to have enough body, and I look pale. Even my new blouse looks awful — it's too big and makes my flat chest look even flatter. If only I had bigger breasts. I open the medicine cabinet and take out the new tube of brown lipstick. I put some more on, relishing its cosmetic taste. I rub two spots into my cheeks. There. Now I look healthier. I tease my hair, trying to make it stand up from my scalp. It's hopeless. In the mirror, I can see one of Hilary's bras hanging over the edge of the laundry bin behind me. Suddenly I have a brainstorm. Why didn't I think of it before? I tear off my blouse and put on the bra. I stuff the cups with toilet paper and button up my blouse again. I turn in front of the mirror and feel satisfied. Now I can go downstairs and face everyone.

Stacy Jones and Phoebe Ness have arrived, with Phoebe's brother Sidney and a short, squat kid named Oliver Potts. Oliver lives next door to Phoebe and is a day student at Middletown Prep. I like him immediately. He looks sort of like a bumblebee. He's wearing a black and yellow rugby shirt and has black, curly hair that he wears Afro style. He also has on white sneakers that have red hearts painted all over them.

We sit down on Hilary's mother's L-shaped couch. Hilary puts on some country and western music. There's a dish of pâté and some shrimp on the table. Couldn't Hilary's mother settle for pretzels and potato chips just once?

I ask Stacy how her five brothers are.

"Awful," says Stacy, and she tells me about how her youngest brother put a dead goldfish on her plate at breakfast.

Oliver Potts bursts into giggles. "I'll have to try that on my sister."

Maybe he's not so cool after all.

"If Sidney did that to me, I'd kill him," says Phoebe, and she elbows Sidney in the ribs.

Sidney punches her back.

"Creep," says Phoebe, and she puts an ice cube down the front of his shirt.

Meanwhile, Dick, Rick, and Oliver turn on the TV. Sidney, Phoebe, and Stacy follow them, and Julie goes upstairs to the bathroom. So I'm left alone on the sofa with Hilary, Boots, and Sam Fraker.

Boots puts his arm around Hilary, and they start whispering to each other.

Sam is sitting at the end of the couch looking through a copy of *Sports Illustrated*. Every now and then, he talks to Hilary and Boots about the Middletown Prep football game he played in that afternoon. I just sit there, feeling like a lump.

Finally I screw up my courage and say, "Do you play a lot of football?"

"I'm the center," Sam says, looking at me as if I'm a clod of dirt unstuck from the cleats of his shoe.

"Oh," I mumble, wishing I could disappear into the cushions behind me.

"You're new in town, huh?" he says.

Thank goodness he's asked me a question.

"I've lived here all my life," I say, "but I switched schools this year, and now I'm at Miss Pringle's."

I try to keep my voice from quivering. Sam moves closer to me on the couch.

"Do you like it?" he asks.

"It sure is different," I say. "There's a lot of homework, but the teachers are good. Where do you come from?"

"Baltimore, Maryland," he says. "Hey, you've got really nice blue eyes. Sort of like my sister's."

I feel myself turn red as a fire engine. Sam moves closer and puts his arm around me. I feel the toilet paper move against my chest as I lean forward, reaching for the shrimp. I wish Sam would take his arm away, but he doesn't, so I stand up and say, "Let's go watch TV."

Just then Hilary's mother comes in with some china plates. Fred follows her with a tray of silverware and napkins. It looks like he might drop the tray any second, it's so big. Poor kid. Next Hilary's mother brings in a huge salad and a platter of steaming coq au vin. It smells delicious.

"Chow time," yells Hilary's mother.

She sure is making a big deal over a little party. Mom would have just ordered in pizzas and Coke. I think it's kind of strange to go to all of this trouble.

"Another of your mother's delicious meals," says Boots.

"Good-bye to Middletown Prep leather meat specials. Can I move in?" adds Sam. How dumb.

We all pile our plates with food and go sit on the floor in the living room. Oliver Potts comes over to where I've nudged myself into a corner and says, "Mind if I sit down?"

"No, go ahead."

He has three pieces of chicken on his plate and several pieces of French bread. No wonder he's sort of squashy looking.

"Do you like animals?" he asks.

"Yep. I have a Newfoundland named Napoleon, and I'd have cats, too, if my dad wasn't allergic."

"My dad's allergic, too," says Oliver.

"Do you have any pets?" I ask.

"A boa constrictor, an iguana, and a hermit crab," he answers.

"Wow. How big is the boa constrictor?"

"About four feet. He's not big enough to hurt you."

"What do you feed him?"

"A live rat every other week."

"Yuck."

Just then Hilary puts on some disco music.

Oliver Potts starts moving back and forth to the beat, and the hearts on his sneakers jump up and down.

"Do you like to dance?" he asks. I don't want to admit that I've never tried, so I simply say, "No, not really. I just like to watch."

"I've been taking disco lessons," says

Oliver. "It's really fun. Do you want to learn?"

But just as I'm thinking about *what* I want, Sam Fraker grabs my arm and pulls me out of my corner and up off the floor.

"Come on, let's dance," he says.

Before I have a chance to protest, he starts whirling me around. My feet stick to the rug like cookie dough, but after a few minutes, they begin to move in time with the music.

"Hey," says Hilary, as she and Boots dance by, "you look like John Travolta and Olivia Newton-John."

The next song is slower, and Sam puts his big hand on my back and presses me close as we move around the floor. I feel nervous, since I've never been this close to a male in my whole life. Oh, sure, I've hugged Dad and Jonah lots of times, but that's different from dancing slowly with somebody who's fifteen years old. I wonder if he can tell that I have toilet paper in my bra. For a moment I see Oliver gliding by with Julie. They look sort of neat together with their plump bodies and curly hair, rocking to the music. Julie gives me a dirty look. I wonder if she has a crush on Sam.

Hilary turns the lights out, and I can tell that she and Boots are making out over on the couch. Sam puts both his arms around me and starts to kiss the top of my head. Yuck. I want to tell him to stop, but I'm scared I'll hurt his feelings. I just let him keep kissing me. I don't know what he finds so exciting about a bunch of hair in his mouth, but that's all right with me, as long as he doesn't try to kiss me on the mouth. He does. He takes his hand and lifts up my chin and kisses me right on the lips. Then he tries to stick his tongue between my teeth. It feels really gross. I think I'm going to throw up.

15. Slumber Party

"I'll be right back," I say, as I dash from the room. I just make it to the bathroom in time to lose all of Hilary's mother's coq au vin in the toliet. My throat is raw, and my eyes are parched and red, but I feel much better. I open the window and lean out to get some fresh air.

Why couldn't I tell that creepy Sam Fraker to lay off? Why do I care what he and his stupid friends think of me? I hate this party. I undo my blouse and tear off Hilary's bra. I use the crumpled toilet paper to wipe my face. I wash off the eye shadow, put on some fresh lipstick, give my hair a quick brush, and open the bathroom door.

Oliver Potts is standing in the hall.

"Are you all right?" he asks.

"Sure," I lie. "Just a little sick from the

coq au vin. My dad's allergic to cats, but I'm allergic to fancy food, I guess."

"I wish *I* was," says Oliver Potts. "Then maybe I'd lose some weight."

He laughs a low, hoarse laugh that sounds like a foghorn. "Will you dance with me now?"

"All right," I say.

We stay in the hall outside the bathroom while he shows me some disco steps. It's actually sort of fun, especially because I don't feel like he's pressuring me.

At eleven o'clock, people's parents start to arrive. Mrs. Ness comes to pick up Phoebe, Sidney, and Oliver.

"It sure was nice meeting you," says Oliver. "Maybe sometime we can get together and go to a movie or something."

Good grief. I'm blushing. As usual. Why can't I be cool like Hilary?

"Sure," I say, picking at the bottom of my lip with my fingers. I've probably smeared lipstick all over my teeth.

Mrs. Harwood comes into the living room, and Hilary and Boots spring apart. It's lucky that she hasn't seen them stuck together like two barnacles all evening.

"It's time for me to take the boys back to Middletown Prep," she says.

"Aw, do we have to go so early?" asks Boots.

"You know the rules," says Mrs. Harwood.

After a bunch of good-byes that seems to go on forever, they leave. Julie and Stacy are staying at Hilary's for the night also, so we all go up to Hilary's bedroom.

Since there are only two beds, Stacy and I have to sleep in sleeping bags on the floor.

Stacy puts her hair in rollers. I don't know how she can stand it. She must feel like a pincushion when she wakes up in the morning.

"Do you want to use some of my skin cleanser?" she asks.

"Thanks," I say. Even though I've never used it, I figure it will make it easier to wipe off what's left of the lipstick on my cheeks. After all, I don't want to soil any of Hilary's mother's monogrammed towels.

"I think Oliver really likes you," says Julie.

"He's silly," I say, "but I had fun talking to him. He owns a boa constrictor."

"Gross," says Stacy, grimacing. "What if it ever got loose?"

Hilary slips on her black nightgown, and poses in front of the mirror. "Boots wants me to come visit his family during Christmas vacation."

"You lucky," says Stacy. "Where does his family live?"

"They own six houses in Europe and the United States. They are spending Christmas at their house in Aspen, Colorado. Skiing," she adds.

"But you don't even know how to ski!" says Julie.

"Not knowing how to do something has never stopped me before," says Hilary. "I'll just have to learn once I get out there."

Hilary sits down on the bed and starts to paint her toenails bright red. Now, who's ever going to see painted toenails at this time of year? Not all her beauty ideas make sense.

"Where was Sam all evening?" she asks. "He disappeared after dancing with Laurie."

Julie looks at me smugly. "He ended up with *me* on the terrace. It was really cold — but I didn't mind." Julie wraps her arms around her middle. So she does like Sam.

"Nice going," says Hilary.

"I didn't get much dinner," says Julie. "I'm hungry!"

"You must have worked up quite an appetite out on the terrace," says Stacy, laughing.

Julie throws a pillow at her. Then she says, "I wish we could order in a pizza!"

Hilary looks at me. "Speaking of pizzas. . . ."

Oh, no. I was hoping that she wouldn't remember about yesterday. Everyone's eyes are on me. I feel like a mouse about to be pounced on by three cats.

"You and Soap were up to something," says Hilary. "I know you weren't at that pizza place."

I feel myself beginning to weaken.

"Where were you? Hiding alarm clocks in the French room?" asks Julie.

How'd she find out about that?

"Or putting Saran Wrap on the toilets in the bathroom?" asks Hilary.

"Or letting the air out of the tires in the faculty parking lot?" asks Stacy.

Hilary must have told them everything. I wish they'd stop. I don't want to tell.

"Come on. Tell. We won't breathe a word to anyone," urges Hilary.

The three of them sit silently. I can feel Soap's secret on the tip of my tongue.

"Please?" coaxes Julie.

I look down at my hands. I can't help myself now. I can feel the words slipping out of me.

"We were at Rayburn Park," I say. "Spying on Soap's father."

"Why on earth were you doing that?" asks Hilary.

"You promise you won't tell?"

Hilary rolls her eyes toward the ceiling. "Honestly. Of course we won't."

"Do you all promise?"

Everyone promises.

"Okay. Mr. Solokoff is having an affair with . . . Miss Helms!"

There, I said it. Everyone gasps. My stomach is one big, hard knot.

"You're kidding!" says Hilary, after she finds her voice. "Tell us what happened."

So I tell them the whole story, while they sit around me, gulping down every word. They ask a billion questions. Like what Miss Helms was wearing. And what she and Mr. Sokoloff talked about. And if they kissed. I try and answer everything, except I don't tell them about Soap crying.

The hard knot in my stomach begins to loosen and I enjoy being the center of attention. But only for a few minutes. The knot comes back. Soap had asked me not to tell, and I had done it. "My whole life is falling apart, and you're the only person I can turn to," she had said. The knot in my stomach grows tighter.

Everyone goes to sleep but me. I change position a hundred times inside the sleeping bag. One minute it's too hot. The next it's too cold. And I can't shut my mind off. All I can think about is the ugly, horrible monster I've become. I wish I knew what to do. Only a few days ago I thought about getting rid of Soap. Now I don't want to. I feel like I'll never be close to Hilary. She's too old for me and when I try to be like her, I feel fake. It's more important than ever that I stay friends with Soap. I don't want to hurt her. I can't tell her what I did. She'd never understand and she'd never speak to me again.

I turn over. I don't have to go to choir practice because of the slumber party, so I won't see her in church tomorrow.

16. Soap Finds Out

On Monday Miss Helms asks us to hand in our autobiographies. Everyone does except Soap. She just sits there and glares at Miss Helms. I can hear a tiny nervous twitch in Miss Helms' voice as she says, "Lucinda, could you see me after class, please?"

Julie whispers something to Hilary, and they giggle.

Thank goodness Soap doesn't hear them. She looks over at me, but I look away. I can't look her in the eye. She called me yesterday, but I told Mom and Dad to tell her I'd call her back. Except I never did.

I wonder if Mr. Sokoloff has told Soap's mother about Miss Helms. How can Soap and Miss Helms be in the same room with each other without having nervous break-downs?

Soap asks me to sit with her at lunch. So do Julie and Hilary and Stacy and Phoebe.

But I sit with Soap. If I avoid her any longer, she'll know something's wrong.

I feel this big space between us, but she doesn't seem to notice. And she doesn't talk about her father. Or Miss Helms. Or her mother. She just rattles on and on about her history project. She's decided to write about P. T. Barnum of Barnum and Bailey Circus. Then she tells me about how she has to go to New York City with her mother on the Saturday of Thanksgiving weekend to have lunch with her Aunt Beatrice. That's when Mr. Sokoloff is planning to meet Miss Helms in Boston.

"So your mother doesn't know yet about Miss Helms?"

"Nope. Pops hasn't told her."

"What did Miss Helms say to you after class?"

"She wanted to know why I hadn't handed in my autobiography."

"Wasn't it sort of awkward? What'd you tell her?"

"I told her that I didn't want her to know about my life."

"Soap!"

"It's none of her business."

"You might flunk."

"I don't care."

While we're eating, everyone at Hilary's table is talking in low, excited voices and staring at Soap. I know what they're talking about, and I am scared and angry. Miss Helms walks through the cafeteria to the faculty dining room, and they all start giggling. To my horror, Julie stands up and hugs herself, making kissing noises. Soap turns around and looks. Hilary immediately grabs Julie and pulls her down to her chair, but it's too late. Soap turns white as a ghost. I think she's going to faint.

"You told," she hisses. "How could you?"

Before I can answer, she gets up and runs out of the room.

I run after her to the bathroom, where she's locked herself in.

I knock several times.

"Go away," she yells. "I don't want to talk to you."

"But I want to explain," I say.

"I don't want to hear about it."

"Please!"

"I hate you."

I don't blame her. I hate myself, too, and Hilary and Julie and the others. I knock on the door again, but Soap won't unlock it. How am I ever going to get through the rest of the afternoon?

Soap doesn't look at me or anyone else during history class. She just stares stubbornly at her work with this hostile, hurt expression on her face. I feel her pain, and at the same time there's a volcano inside me.

Soap doesn't come to school for the next two days. Hilary acts as if nothing has happened. We have a sort of fake friendship. Everything's on the surface, and I want to get what's underneath out in the open. But I can't yet. Not until I work things through with Soap. Anyway, Hilary and I have to keep peace until we finish our report for Mr. Bernstein. It's due right after Thanksgiving break.

We get out of school early on that Wednesday. Hilary invites me over to her house to talk about our project, but I tell her to come to my house instead. I want to be home when Jonah arrives, and besides, Hilary's always wanted to meet him.

Hilary has finished all of her research on Victoria Woodhull and wants to read me her notes. She's dug up a lot of interesting information, like the fact that Victoria Woodhull was unpopular with other suffragists. They didn't share her views on free love or marriage. She didn't think a husband and wife had to be faithful. I guess Victoria Woodhull would think it's wonderful that Mr. Sokoloff and Miss Helms are having an affair. But of course that's the one subject we can't talk about.

After Hilary reads me her information, I read her what I've found out about Susan B. Anthony. She started off as a schoolteacher and went around the country hundreds of times to preach about equal rights.

While we're working, I hear a car come in the driveway. Then the front door opens. Jonah! I rush downstairs and throw myself into his arms.

"Hey, little sister," he says. "How're you doing?" He picks me up and whirls me around. I feel his glasses slide down to the tip of his nose as he kisses me. Napoleon jumps all over him, wiggling back and forth like some huge fish that's just been caught.

"Who's your friend?" asks Jonah as he sees Hilary standing at the bottom of the stairs.

"Oh, um, this is Hilary. Hilary, this is Jonah."

Hilary smiles her movie-star smile, the one where all her teeth show. She reaches out her hand and says, "So I've finally met the great Jonah Endersby."

"Yep, the one and only Jonah Endersby, famous for being Laurie's brother."

I giggle. I'm mostly known in town as Jonah's sister, so it's kind of nice to hear Jonah switch things around.

"Where's Mom and Dad?" asks Jonah.

Just then the Volvo turns into the driveway and comes to a screeching halt. Gravel flies everywhere. Mom's driving, of course. Dad puts his hands over his face as if he thinks they're going to crash. Dad likes to tease Mom about reckless driving.

After all the hugging is over, we sit around the kitchen table sipping hot chocolate. Jonah tells us about college. He plays a lot of sports, like soccer, and has a terrific political science course. Naturally, he's getting straight As. Dad and Mom look at him worshipfully, as usual, but I don't feel jealous. After all, they haven't seen him for two months.

Hilary hardly says a word. She just sits and watches Jonah, and laughs her bubbly laugh whenever he makes a joke.

Every now and then, Jonah glances at her and smiles with half of his mouth. He always smiles that funny half smile when he's really happy.

I sit and watch both of them. It's strange. I don't feel mad at Hilary anymore. It wasn't really her fault that Soap found out. Julie's the one who screwed things up by making those dumb kissing noises. Anyway, I'm mostly mad at myself. I'm the one who spilled the beans.

I wonder why Soap didn't come to school. Did her mother find out? Will Soap forgive me? Will I ever learn to keep my mouth shut?

Before Hilary leaves to go to her house for dinner, she asks me what I'm doing Friday night. She and Boots have a date since his parents are in Europe, and he has to stay at Middletown Prep for Thanksgiving. He has some guy he wants me to meet, and Hilary wants us to go out together.

I guess I want to go, but I wonder if my parents will let me. I'll have to wait and ask them when they're in a really good mood.

17. Thanksgiving

On Thanksgiving morning, we all get up early and make a big, fancy breakfast. On holidays, we always eat homemade biscuits, scrambled eggs with lots of spices in them, sausages, and fresh-squeezed orange juice. Dad makes the eggs, Jonah fries the sausages, and I make the biscuits and squeeze the orange juice. Mom is busy stuffing the turkey. It goes in the oven early and will finish cooking while we're in church at a special Thanksgiving service.

"You're not going to wear pants, are you?" asks Dad. He stares at my green corduroy Levi's, which I've put on precisely because I *was* planning to wear them to church. I've never understood why Dad gets so uptight when I don't wear a skirt.

"Why shouldn't I? No one's going to see them under my choir robe."

"Because they're not dressy enough. I

don't want you looking like a tramp."

"Oh, honestly, everyone wears pants to choir. I'm not going to wear a skirt. It'd be ridiculous."

Sometimes Dad is so old-fashioned, I can't believe it. I look over at Mom, but she hasn't been listening. Her attention is on the turkey, and she's not doing a very good job, either. Gobs of stuffing are on the floor. I shrug my shoulders. What's the point of making a big scene on Thanksgiving?

"Okay. I'll change before we leave," I say.

Soap doesn't show up for choir practice. For a moment, I wonder whether she's done something drastic, like run away or poison herself. But that's silly. She's probably just sick or thinks she might get sick if she gets within two feet of me.

Mr. Whitten waves his arms around and gets us to sing "We Gather Together" as loudly as we can. If only I could think of something to be thankful for. Right now I don't feel thankful about anything.

As I look out over the congregation, I see Mom and Dad and Jonah sitting in the fourth row. Mom looks nice in the new yellow suit that Dad bought her, and Dad's hair is smoothed down. It looks like he's polished it with shoe wax. A few rows behind them, I see Mrs. Sokoloff. My stomach jumps. Soap is next to her, all bent over as if she's praying. Mr. Sokoloff isn't with them. Even though he's Jewish, he's always been in church on Thanksgiving Day. Probably because his wife has made him go. Mrs. Sokoloff takes a handkerchief out of her suit pocket and dabs her eyes. Good grief, she must have found out! She's not acting like herself. Usually she sits in church and stares straight ahead. I try to imagine Mr. Sokoloff telling Soap's mother about his affair:

MR. SOKOLOFF: Bernice, I have something terrible to tell you.

MRS. SOKOLOFF: Did you overdraw our account again?

MR. SOKOLOFF: No. Now, I want you to sit down. (I can picture Mr. Sokoloff's Adam's apple going up and down like some yo-yo.)

MRS. SOKOLOFF: Why do I have to sit down? Hurry up and tell me. I have to get to a hair appointment.

MR. SOKOLOFF: I'm in love with Soap's English teacher.

MRS. SOKOLOFF: You're *what*????????

Soap looks up, and I catch her eye for a second. She doesn't smile or give me any signal. Her face is blank. My stomach knots up and I look away.

* * *

On the way home, I have visions of the turkey and gravy and stuffing and sweet potatoes and wild rice and beans and creamed onions and cranberry sauce. But when we get into the house, Mom looks puzzled.

"I don't smell the turkey," she says. Then she dashes into the kitchen. We dash in after her.

"Oh, no, I forgot to turn the oven on!"

"Mom, how could you?" asks Jonah.

Dad looks disappointed. Then he bursts into laughter. "This isn't the first time you've forgotten something. Remember the time you forgot your wallet, and you had to spend the night in the railroad station in Pittsburgh?"

Soon we are all remembering the times Mom has forgotten things. Dad gets out a bottle of wine, and Jonah and I heat up the vegetables. We sit around the kitchen table eating the best vegetarian meal of our lives!

Since everyone is feeling so rosy, I decide to ask about tomorrow night's date.

"Um, Dad, Mom, is it okay with you if I go on a date tomorrow night? Hilary has this boyfriend named Boots who goes to Middletown Prep, and he has a friend he wants to fix me up with."

Mom stops laughing for a moment to

look at me. It's as if she's noticing something different for the first time. A tiny little frown begins to form around her eyes.

Dad sets his wine glass down on the table.

"How old is Boots' friend?"

"Around fifteen or so," I answer. "Boots is really nice. I met him at Hilary's party."

"You're too young to go out on a date with a fifteen-year-old," says Dad. "Maybe your mother and I will feel differently next year. But right now it's out of the question."

I feel like I've just been punched in the stomach. How dare he talk to me like that? Doesn't he trust me? I look over at Mom. She shrugs her shoulders.

"I agree with your father," she says.

Typical.

I look at Jonah. He raises his eyes to the ceiling in an aren't-they-impossible look. But at least he says something.

"What are you scared of? Laurie can take care of herself. What can a couple of kids do that's so terrible?"

"Lots of things," says Dad. "You haven't forgotten that only a month ago, Laurie and Soap got suspended from school."

"I think you're making a big deal over nothing," says Jonah. "Hilary's different from Soap. She and Laurie won't get into trouble."

"Different troubles, yes," says Dad.

He blots his mouth with his napkin and starts to get up from the table.

"I think Jonah has a point," says Mom. Hey, good for Mom. "Hilary is a nice girl, and if Laurie's home by eleven o'clock, I don't think we should worry."

"That's right, Dad. I'll even pick them up at the theater," says Jonah.

"Well, that changes things," says Dad. He throws up his hands. "I give up." Then he sits down and pours himself another glass of wine. He lifts it up and says, "Here's to Laurie and her mystery date. May he be tall, handsome, and smart!"

I give them all a hug and waltz up to bed. The only thing that keeps it from being a perfect evening is the heavy feeling I have when I think about Soap. I wish it would go away.

18. Blind Date

Boots' friend is from Florida, and his name is Anthony Roberts. He's tall with wavy hair and a very wispy mustache. We stop in Ken's Coffee Shop for milk shakes before the movie, and Anthony describes the trip he and his father take every spring to collect tropical fish. Of course Hilary, being a fish freak, chats right along.

"Do you use a slurp gun?" she asks.

Now how does she know about slurp guns?

"Nah. We use nets, and sea urchins for bait. We crush the urchins with a stick and wait for the fish to eat the meat. Then we scoop up the ones we want with our net."

"Do you have a salt-water aquarium?" asks Hilary.

"No. I usually throw them back in the water."

Why does he even bother to catch them

if he's just going to get rid of them? How dumb.

"You should get yourself an aquarium," says Hilary. "I have one in my room. I have to get special chemicals from the pet store to make sure the water is salty enough for the tropical fish my father sends me every Christmas."

"Hey, maybe sometime I can come look at them."

Boots gives Anthony a dirty look.

"Sure," says Hilary. "I have an angelfish, and a damselfish, and a. . . ."

Sometimes I wish Hilary would shut up. Otherwise, how can a person get a word in edgewise? Not that I have anything interesting to say. I look over at Boots. He's drumming his fingers on the table and looking bored.

"When do your parents get back from Europe?" I ask him.

"I don't know," he says.

He doesn't add anything else, and I can't think of what to say next, so I'm relieved when he looks at his watch and says it's time to leave.

As we walk up Main Street to the Gilbert Theater, Boots pulls out a cigarette and lights it. It smells funny. Different. Good grief, it's not a cigarette. It's marijuana.

"Do you want some?" he asks, trying to sound casual, and passes it to Hilary.

Hilary looks over at me with an I'll-do-it-if-you-do-it look. But I don't want to. It scares me, and besides, I'm nervous about walking up Main Street in full view of the police and everybody. I look away.

Hilary giggles nervously and takes the joint. "My mother would kill me if she knew I was doing this," she says. She sucks in a huge drag. Her face gets red as she holds the smoke in her chest, and I can tell that she's trying hard not to cough. I guess she really wants to impress Boots.

Hilary passes the joint to Anthony. It's obvious he's smoked a lot of dope, since he sucks it down like a real pro. He doesn't even get red in the face or cough or anything. Then he passes it to me. Everyone's looking at me. I don't want to smoke it, but I'm in the same old dilemma. If I say no, they'll laugh at me. I may lose Hilary as a friend. I take the joint. I suck the smoke toward the back of my throat and try to swallow it. It tastes terrible, and my throat feels like a furnace. Suddenly I start coughing and my eyes get all watery.

"Haven't you ever gotten high?" asks Anthony. I hate the superior tone in his voice.

"Lots of times," I say in a squeaky voice.

"It's just that this is really strong stuff."

I suck in another drag and force myself to breathe it down to my chest. Even though I feel like coughing, I hold it back. Hilary's looking at me, and for a moment, she looks as if she's sorry. But then she laughs and says, "I feel good. Let me have some more."

So the four of us get stoned. I'm terrified that the cops are going to arrest us. I feel sick to my stomach, I'm so scared. I hate this date. I feel dizzy and lean against the wall of the theater as we wait in line to get our tickets. It helps. Maybe if I'm very quiet and concentrate on getting control of myself, I'll be okay.

After we pay for our tickets and go inside, Boots makes a beeline for the candy and popcorn counter. He buys Goobers and M&Ms and Jordan Almonds and Jujubes and Chuckles and four king-sized tubs of popcorn. I have to admit that I'm suddenly starving. I can't wait to eat. I tear off the Chuckles wrapper.

Boots wants to sit in the back row, probably so he and Hilary can make out. We fall over about ten people as we stumble toward the seats farthest in. The movie hasn't started yet, and everyone seems to be watching us. I'm sure that we look very strange, and I try to look as serious as possible so no one will think anything's wrong. Hilary keeps giggling, and one lady says, "Shhhh."

After we sit down, Anthony puts his arm around me. Yuck. As I lean in the other direction, I see a familiar shape walking down the aisle toward the front row. My goodness, it's Oliver Potts! And he's with Phoebe and her brother Sidney. I don't want Oliver to see me. I sink down lower into my seat, and Anthony leans over to whisper something in my ear.

"Do you want a Coke?"

Do I ever. My throat is parched, and my body feels like a desert.

Anthony stumbles over the ten people again, and they start complaining and whispering to each other.

The movie is a science-fiction film with lots of special effects and weird music. I can hear each musical instrument, and the screen ripples with pink, purple, and orange colors. Maybe this is what people like about grass. But I still don't like the feeling of being out of control. I feel like I'm way up high some place.

As I watch the movie, I almost forget about Anthony until his fingers start going up and down my back, like I'm a cello. I lean forward, and he puts his hand on my shoulder. Then he brushes my hair back and starts kissing my ear. I pull away, hoping he'll get the hint and stop. I don't want to make out. Hilary and Boots are hugging and kissing, and both of Boots' hands are on her back. I wonder if he's trying to undo her bra.

"What's wrong?" asks Anthony.

"I want to watch the movie," I say. I'm getting angry.

"That's no fun," says Anthony. Then he tries to kiss me again. I can feel his hot breath on my face. Can't boys think about anything except making out?

I feel like socking him.

He doesn't do anything for a few minutes, but then he puts his hand on my leg.

I have to get away from him. I don't care if Hilary never speaks to me again. She's no friend of mine if she's fixed me up with a creep like this.

I stand up and grab my jacket.

"I'm leaving," I say.

For one second, Hilary looks up.

"What's wrong?"

"Everything."

"Don't pay any attention to her," says Boots.

"Shhhhhh." It seems like everyone in the audience can hear us. But I don't care anymore. I really don't care. I turn my back on all of them and march out of the theater. Then I burst into tears.

I call Jonah from the pay phone on the corner. Luckily, he's home and can come pick me up.

19. I Talk to Jonah

I don't say anything. I just hunch against the door as Jonah drives.

"What's wrong with you?" he asks very gently. "Why the tears?"

"The guy Hilary fixed me up with was awful. And I smoked some grass, which I hated. And Soap hates me. And now Hilary hates me, but I don't care."

"Hey, slow down. Why don't you tell me everything from the beginning?" says Jonah as he pulls into our driveway. He shuts off the motor and turns to look at me. His head and glasses and neck make a perfect silhouette in the light from our porch.

But I can't talk to him yet. I want to be alone for a while. "Later," I say. "After I've had some time to think. I'm going to my room."

Jonah shrugs. "Okay." Then we both get out of the car.

I don't even bother to put on my pajamas. I just lie on my bed in my underwear and cry into my pillow. Why do I feel so miserable? Isn't it good I stood up for myself? Finally? Or should I have pretended I was having a good time and acted grown up and sophisticated like Hilary, even if I was feeling rotten inside? I need Hilary as a friend, especially now that I've lost Soap. Or do I? I don't know what I want.

Suddenly there is a knock on the door.

"It's me," says Jonah. "Can I come in?"

I roll over and stare at the wall. Maybe I *should* talk to Jonah. Maybe he can help me.

"Just a minute."

I put on my bathrobe, unlock the door, and stand to the side so he can come in. My hair's a mess, and I'm all puffy from crying.

"I brought you some peppermint tea," says Jonah. "I thought it might make you feel better."

"Thanks."

We sit down next to each other on the bed, and I start sipping the tea. The warm candy flavor feels good as it trickles down my throat.

"Now do you want to tell me what happened?" asks Jonah. His voice is soothing. He really wants to help.

So I tell him about Hilary and her party and my date with Anthony, and then I tell him about Soap and her father and his affair with Miss Helms and how I told Hilary and the others her secret. I tell him everything.

Jonah's quiet for a while. He takes off his glasses and rubs his eyes. He whistles softly. "Phew. That's quite a load, Laurie." I start crying. "Soap's old man has got himself another woman, huh? That's really far-out."

Is that all Jonah can say after I've spilled my guts to him?

"Do you think it was all right that I left the movie?" I ask.

Jonah chews on the earpiece of his glasses for a second. He always does that when he's thinking.

"Yeah," he says. "I think Anthony sounds like a typical sex-crazed Middletown preppie. Anyway, Hilary was thinking more about making Boots happy by fixing up his friend than about you."

I think back to how Hilary smoked grass just to impress Boots. She was just as scared inside as me. So she's not perfect either. Suddenly I feel a lot better.

"Do you think Soap will ever speak to me again?"

"Sure," says Jonah. "She's just going

through a lot of changes right now. Heavy changes."

I have a feeling Jonah's wrong. I don't think Soap wants to be my friend anymore.

"Why is it so hard for me to say no?"

"I guess we all want to be liked," says Jonah. "We're afraid we won't be if we go against what's popular."

"Do you feel that way?"

"Of course," says Jonah. "But you have to be honest with yourself and with your friends. Otherwise, people won't respect you. Like, if you don't stick up for what you. . . ."

I can tell that Jonah's winding up to give me a lecture. But I don't want to hear it. I want to be alone. I have to figure out how to get back with Soap. I don't want to lose her.

"Jonah? Do you mind if we talk another time? I'm getting really sleepy."

Jonah looks the tiniest bit hurt. But just for a second. He gets up and his fist touches my chin.

"Sure, little sister. I'll see you tomorrow, huh?"

I lie awake a long time after the door closes. It feels good knowing I don't like Hilary as much as I thought. She's really selfish. And without her fancy clothes and makeup and dates, she'd be boring. At least compared to Soap. Soap doesn't need all that stuff to be interesting. She already is, and I miss her. So how can I make her understand what I did?

I turn on the light and shuffle over to the window. Maybe if I write her a letter. . . . I find some legal-pad paper and a purple Magic Marker.

Dear Soap,
    I've been feeling rotten inside. Can you forgive me?
                        Love,
                        Laurie

Dear Soap,
    Ever since you found out I told Hilary about your father, I've been feeling about one inch tall. I am really, really sorry. See, I didn't mean to do it. It's just that I've always had a hard time saying no. Hilary and Julie and Stacy pressured me into telling them — and I couldn't help myself. But I don't feel that way anymore. I don't even like them that much. But I miss you. I want to be friends again.
                        Love,
                        Laurie

After two tries, I finally decide that I really need to *talk* to Soap. So I write:

Dear Soap,

Can you meet me in church when you get back from visiting your Aunt Beatrice Saturday afternoon? At about six o'clock? *Please?* I know you're mad at me, but I have to talk to you. I am really, really sorry about what happened.

Love,
Laurie

The next day, I leave the note in her mailbox so that she'll get it when she gets back from New York.

20. "Heart and Soul"

I don't know about Soap. It's seven o'clock, and she still isn't here. The church is dark and cold. I tiptoe up to the altar and walk back and forth to keep warm.

Finally I hear the door open. Soap's familiar shape emerges from the shadows, and the hollow sound of her clogs echoes through the church as she walks up the aisle.

"Soap!" I yell.

"Laurie!" She walks more quickly but then slows down. And stops at the bottom of the steps that lead up to the altar. She seems scared to come closer.

"Are you still mad at me?" I ask.

"Not as much."

I start telling her right away about what happened. "When I was spending the night at Hilary's, Stacy and Julie were there, and they kept bugging me about where we were last Friday, and I couldn't help myself. See, I have this problem about saying no. I didn't want to tell them, but I couldn't help it. Can you understand?"

Soap comes up the steps, and we both sit down.

She rubs her hands together to warm them and leans against a pillar.

"I guess I believe you didn't mean to, but it's hard for me to understand. See, I wouldn't ever do that to you. But . . . it doesn't matter now."

"What do you mean?"

"It's not a secret anymore. Now that my father's told my mother, everyone will find out anyway."

"When did he tell her?"

"He told her after I went to bed Wednesday night. He was gone when I woke up Thanksgiving morning. It made me angry. And I was already angry about everything in general, which is why I stayed home from school. My mother's really upset. She's been crying a lot."

"Do you think your father will stay in Middletown?"

"I don't know. I'm actually more worried about my mother. But you know what? Ever since this happened, she's been different. Softer and, well, nicer."

Soap stands up.

"Hey, my fingers are cold. Do you want to play the organ?"

"Sure."

Soap goes up to the organ and sits down. She flicks the switch and starts playing the top part of "Heart and Soul." I sit down beside her and lift my fingers to the keys. I feel this great sense of relief. As we play, our music fills the hollow spaces in the church.

I think about everything that's happened. About how Hilary isn't as great as I once thought. About how Soap's changing, like Jonah said. About how maybe I'm changing, too. About all the things I have to look forward to. Maybe even Oliver Potts.

About the Author

Margery Cuyler grew up in Princeton, New Jersey, and was graduated from Sarah Lawrence College. She is a children's book editor, and author of *Jewish Holidays* and *The All-Around Pumpkin Book*. She lives in Rowayton, Connecticut, with her husband, Jan. *The Trouble with Soap* is her first novel.